Book Three of the Endless Breath Saga

A Roar
Through Time

Nicholas Licalsi

STEP INTO THE ROAD

For Charlie. Hope this book can question some of your answers.

Thank You Patrons!

Thank You Patrons!

There's nothing quite like the magic of exploring new worlds and
meeting unique characters through storytelling.
And there's *absolutely* nothing like the magic of knowing that there
are people willing to support that expedition.
This story is my bounty. I hope you enjoy it.

Katelyn Combs, Bonnie Adams, BW, Melinda Callender,
Roy & Beth Shockey, Sam Meeks, John Middleton, Matt VanNatten.

Join the crew at: https://patreon.com/stepintotheroad

1

I pulled up to the mansion in a driverless hovercar. There were a dozen police cruisers parked around the circular drive their red and blue lights flashing in the foggy morning air. It was big news when the head of a conglomerate died and that drew a crowd and authority.

Many citizens of the Central System thought the rich and powerful conglomerate leaders were immortal. After all with their unfathomable power and influence surely a meeting with death could be delayed.

But in most cases citizens were wrong. I'd met generations of Mandlebaums, Wiesmans, and Tichenowas and they were all as mortal as their employees, albeit rich enough to live a century or two longer.

However, in the case of this morning's death, one would be right to say he was immortal. Which was one of the reasons I was so interested in his death.

The other reason was that he was head of the Rungson conglomerate. And up until a few hours ago, I was living in this mansion sleeping peacefully in bed.

Until I was murdered.

The autopilot on the car was having a hard time finding somewhere to land. I could've manually parked it in a small gap between two black and white police cars. I could've used the garage and parked among a dozen other vehicles some archaic others futuristic.

The polished tiled driveway had a stone water fountain in the center with a bronze statue of a stag standing on a rock in its center. The house itself was modern by my standards although the right angles, polished white walls, and large floor-to-ceiling windows might feel antiquated to some citizens of this timeline.

The driveway was lined with well-manicured trees that were tall and slender resembling cypress trees but native to Griffith, the planet I called home in this timeline. Most of the shrubbery around the house was native to Griffith. Exotic species were expensive to import and even more expensive to get approved by the planet's environmental agencies.

To get to the crime scene before any more officials showed up I instructed the computer to park on the grass. My landscaper would have a fit but it'd give him something to do for the week.

Drones buzzed around the sky and the house surveying the area. The police would likely make a 3D model of the area from the drone's data so they could investigate further. I'd be shocked if they found anything useful.

The doors of my car folded open. A small set of stairs extended to the grass. The heat of the hover car's engine filled the wet air with the smell of burnt grass.

I stepped onto the grass, still wet with the morning dew, and it covered my impractical, but allegedly fashionable, raised-heel boots with water. If it was bad for the boot's material I didn't know or care, I could have a dozen replacements here tomorrow.

I was dressed the part of a conglomerate heir. The long robe-like black jacket that nearly reached my ankles was too thin to fight off the chill of the crisp morning. My chaotically patterned shirt underneath it made me look like a tropical bird.

I was grateful that khaki slacks hadn't gone out of fashion in the past few centuries, as they were the only thing I wore that didn't feel ridiculous.

I did wish facial hair would come back in fashion soon. My cleanly shaven cheeks, still a little raw from the rushed job on the shuttle ride here, felt the cold wisp of air that passed by them.

I emerged through the row of thin trees and a half dozen police officers leaped off the rim of the fountain. Until a moment ago they had nothing better to do than sit around and gossip about my death while they waited for the drones to return.

Now that someone was trespassing they could accost me with a dozen meaningless questions about who I was, what I was doing, and if I knew I could be arrested for approaching this house.

I stayed silent until someone finally identified me through their facial recognition program as the heir and owner of this house, land, and planet.

Then everyone went silent.

"Lead me to the head detective please," I finally said.

For a moment no one stepped forward. They were either star-struck or confused by my instructions. I looked at the crowd expectantly. Finally, the short mousy blonde woman who'd identified me as Todd Rungson the V heir to the deceased stepped forward.

"Right this way Mr. Rungson," she said. Using the terminal in her hand she sent off a message and led me up the polished steps to my house.

We passed through the thin glass doors which were rudimentarily held open. Someone had used a rock from the front garden and shoved it in the tracks. I assumed to keep the doors from sliding closed and locking everyone out.

I wish they hadn't been so clever. It'd do less damage to my door, and get these people out of my hair.

The foyer of my mansion was beginning to be filled with bright morning light. A mosaic tile pattern was installed on the floor with two curved marble stairways wrapping around it leading to the second floor.

The officer gestured to an armchair that sat at the edge of the mosaic against the descending stairway. "If you don't mind having a seat Detective Pikowski will be with you shortly."

I gave her my richest and most indignant look. I'm sure my android butler had said the same line to countless guests. But I didn't appreciate being made to wait in my own home.

"I was told my father was found in the bedroom," I said. "I know my way around the house."

"I'd... we'd prefer if you... it's a crime scene," she blurted out unhelpfully.

"I'm aware, hence my eagerness to see it."

"I think it'd be best if you left the investigation to professionals," a woman said from the top of the stairs.

She was not in the timeless blue and black uniform of a police officer. Instead, she wore what passed for fashionable yet practical in this timeline. A faux-leather vest buttoned around a tight-fitting long-sleeve collared shirt. Her loose-fitting slacks were held up by a thick black belt that held a gun, badge, and other utilities of a police officer. Her hair was jet black and cut short with bangs that were remarkably straight and ended just above her eyebrows.

Explaining to her that I had, in at least one or two lifetimes, been a detective would be impossible. I could remind her that I ran the conglomerate that employed her, and was technically her boss, but that didn't seem prudent... yet.

Charm could be effective. But that was not something I was accused of having large quantities of.

"Of course," I said, deciding to go with being helpful. "But I am intimately familiar with my father's habits and tendencies. A set of familiar eyes on the room might help clear up any questions you have about the crime scene. I'm as motivated as you to get to the bottom of this."

Detective Pikowski descended the stairs, the practical flat shoes she wore made a soft patting sound on the marble stairs. Her gaze was fixed on me.

"You're familiar with your father's habits, but we have no record of you ever visiting Griffith until today," she said. "You've spent most of your life on Feldman's station."

She was right. To avoid any complications I always listed my sons as off-world for their entire lives. My heirs only appeared on Griffith when I'd been alive for a suspiciously long time.

"Even worlds apart our family stays close," I said with my best impression of a genuine smile.

"Yet you got here very quickly, considering Feldman's is a few jumps away," the detective stood in front of me as rigid as the posts of the stair's banister.

I could've appeared inside the house, but that would be far too complicated to explain to the police. Instead, I faked some records so it looked like I'd left Feldman's station days before the murder. In reality, I appeared in orbit on a conglomerate satellite this morning.

"He was preparing an important project for the conglomerate and wanted me to be here real time since I was to take it over."

I could hardly consider ordering Gretchen a wardrobe or redesigning the USB from the ground up as important for the conglomerate but those were private records above her pay grade.

She hummed with feigned interest.

"Do you have any leads or ideas about his cause of death?" I asked, genuinely curious. "He was a healthy man, I doubt it was something as trivial as a stroke or heart attack."

Security data for the mansion was stored locally in the building to limit remote tampering but also meant I couldn't check it on the flight down.

"I'm not at liberty to say at this time," the detective replied.

"You are aware that I'll be getting my hands on these crime scene files as soon as they're entered into the system. It'd be easiest for both of us if I was let in sooner rather than later."

"Perhaps," Pikowski said. "But there are proper channels for these things."

"Detective, with all due respect, every one of those proper channels leads back to me." I pulled my hand terminal out of my robe's inner pocket. "Name someone, anyone, I'll give them a call. It'd be career suicide for them to ignore my call or deny my request."

I looked at her expectantly, waiting for a name.

Pikowski sighed in resignation. "Whoever killed your father wanted it to be known that this was a murder. And they altered the security video to make it seem like they could appear and disappear out of thin air."

The first statement about the conspicuous murder of a conglomerate head was concerning. The second sounded unsettlingly familiar and the idea of its consequences sent chills down my spine.

"Whoever did this," Pikowski continued, "was powerful. Extremely powerful. And, with all due respect Mr. Rungson, the most powerful man I can imagine just arrived from Feldman's station. I'd be stupid not to consider him my prime suspect."

I nodded my head and gave Pikowski a thoughtful smile. Accusing the new head of a conglomerate of patricide to his face was bold. I couldn't imagine a better detective to investigate my murder.

Even if the killer was likely capable of far more than she could imagine.

2

I sat on the synth-leather couch in my living room sipping a cup of freshly brewed coffee. It'd been a pain to make the cup, I couldn't find my way around my own kitchen here since my private chef Linda was typically the only one to use it.

But I gave her, and the rest of the staff, a week off to mourn their boss's death. Whether or not they were spending the time mourning or partying was not my concern.

My coffee wasn't bad but more bitter than when Linda brewed it. I sipped it anyway enjoying the familiar taste. As I drank I began to review the security footage on the living room's massive TV.

The living room was almost completely white, like much of the rest of the house. Organics like leather and wood were rare in this, and most of humanity's, future.

Fortunately, anything that came from the ground like clay, granite, marble, and metal was cheap and copious. There were mines for them on world and off. And mining had been automated and profitable ages ago.

Organics like leather and wood took time and resources to nurture and grow. And when humanity was expanding through the stars like bacteria in a Petri dish nurturing luxury items was not a priority.

Society was built on profitable and automatic materials, it was the only way to house so many humans across the Central System. And even with my wealth this house was built and filled with earthen materials.

The side tables, countertops, and the coffee table that my feet currently rested on were all made of white granite speckled with dots of black or silver. The couch was a cushy synth-leather three-seater. An armchair sat to the side of the TV screen in a corner under a lamp with a spherical metal lampshade.

On the other side of the screen was a clay statue taller than me that looked like a snowman halfway through melting and then beaten by a loan shark who hadn't been paid. For the past week I'd been living here I'd considered throwing it off the balcony. This morning was no different.

But that was the cost of having someone else decorate the house. For a world I'd spent so much time in, a world where I was immensely wealthy, I didn't have the sentimental memories to fill this house with anything meaningful. Let alone the countless other homes, starships, and space stations I owned across the Central System. So the work was delegated to a subsidiary of my conglomerate.

Which led to it being filled with artwork that didn't speak to me as much as it screeched an out-of-tune rendition of my least favorite song.

The first viewing of the security footage was jarring. Detective Pikowski, who'd left with the small army of the Griffith police officers a few hours ago, was correct that the killer wanted everyone who saw the security footage to know that this was in fact a murder.

Poison or a dozen different chemicals could've covertly killed me in my sleep. It wouldn't be hard, I ate anything and everything I could get my hands on in this universe. Linda was an amazing chef. Everything she made was worlds better than the freeze-dried stuff on my Fortress of Solitude at the end of the universe.

But no. This killer appeared in the kitchen and grabbed the biggest chef knife they could find. They quietly walked upstairs and sliced my throat. Then, to make sure I was dead, they stabbed me in the chest a few dozen times.

The fact that my master bedroom didn't have a trace of blood in it was a testament to the quality of the crime scene cleaning crew.

The killer wore all black including the rubber-soled sneakers they wore. The jacket had a hood that was pulled up over his head, and a ball cap and bandana made sure everything else was hidden as well. Then the killer disappeared as the detective mentioned.

I restarted the clip watching the killer carefully.

The police department, whose files were being automatically sent to me, had already analyzed the video. Their digital forensics team was unable to get more than the killer's poorly lit eyes. The team, unsurprisingly, had no luck matching the killer with anyone in their facial recognition databases.

The forensic team had also failed to find any evidence of tampering with the data on the recording. A conclusion they refused to accept. Their reports seemed convinced that it was not a matter of *if* the video had been tampered with to make the killer disappear but *how* the tampering was so seamless.

I watched the murder a second time with something else in mind.

After removing the knife from my chest for the twelfth time the killer took a deep breath, then another one. Perhaps they were catching their breath from the work of stabbing me, as most of the police reports claimed. But when the killer disappeared, and the knife fell to the ground with a clatter, there was no doubt in my mind this person could travel the multiverse like me.

So I rewatched it a dozen times, noting their movements, mannerisms, how they walked up the stairs, and what century I thought the clothes might be from.

The killer was right-handed but favored their left foot. The shoes were not a brand I was familiar with, meaning they probably didn't come from a universe I remembered. But the ball cap hasn't been in style since humanity made space travel trivial. Meaning this person was at least as old as me, or favored dressing in the style of the universe I grew up in.

The list of suspects, people I knew could travel the multiverse, wasn't huge. It consisted of me, Gretchen, and a society of avian bird people. The lack of feathers around the killer's eyes eliminated all but two of them.

Gretchen fit the bill. She'd grown up in the same type of universe as me, always wore sneakers, and I couldn't blame her for wanting revenge for me killing so many versions of her across the multiverse.

But we'd made up since then. She forgave me for it and I promised I wouldn't do it again, and would help her escape the tracking memory of the avians.

It could be me, I'd killed myself before. First by an SUV then a few dozen times as an experiment just to see if there was anything that could keep me dead.

My future self had told me, when we met in that coffee shop after my first death, that he'd tried a few different methods and none worked. I made good on his prediction failing to find anything either. And after each death, I woke up in a parallel universe that was almost exactly but not quite an identical image of the previous one.

Which is how I realized I'd been murdered this morning.

I'd finished the project outline for collecting Gretchen's wardrobe over Linda's delicious pancake breakfast. Gretchen had asked for a change of clothes when I left her on the Fortress of Solitude a week ago in my lifetime. With the ability to travel through time, nothing's pressing. There's no urgency when you can disappear and return a moment later after living a lifetime or two.

I'd spent the past week between worlds, the universe I consider my home with its familiar USB technology, and this one where I had my Fortress of Solitude orbiting Jupiter and the red giant that became of the planet's sun.

I couldn't just take notes and email USB's schematics and protocols to myself in this universe. So I had to study it deeply in order to convert it into instructions that the computer on the Fortress would understand.

Luckily nothing is pressing to a time traveler.

The USB information was saved to my personal terminal ready to be sent via a deep space probe to the fortress.

This morning I'd put the final touches on the wardrobe project outline as well. I was preparing to send it to the subsidiary that would curate a fashionable and practical wardrobe for Gretchen in the latest, and by my specific request antiquated, designs. Along with a few practical tools like space suits, mag boots, and astrotherms.

I listed the coordinates in space that it needed to be sent to on the outline. Then to make sure, as the best way to lose something in the multiverse is to send it to the wrong future, I reached out to make sure that I was on the right timeline.

The way I feel the multiverse when I'm traveling through it is like a fraying rope that you can zoom in and out of endlessly without it changing shape, like a fractal. I followed the thread of the universe I was on, ignoring any future fraying it might do. When I found the position in time that my Fortress of Solitude should've existed, with Gretchen on it, I found a lifeless satellite that I'd never visited.

The work order to build and deliver this satellite home I called the Fortress of Solitude was completed by Todd Rungson I. My great great grandfather, according to official records. It existed in the future of every universe that had a Rungson conglomerate. Every time a universe frayed a new Fortress of Solitude was created.

However, I only ever visited one specific version. I only ever shipped supplies to one specific version, and I'd left Gretchen to occupy herself for a few hours, at that one specific version. There was no way to transport goods across the multiverse so shipping a wardrobe of clothes to that universe's future would've been useless to Gretchen.

Which is how I found out I'd woken up in the wrong universe. And the only thing that forced me to travel unexpectedly was death.

My hand terminal rang next to me on the couch shocking me out of my contemplation about the murderer's origins. Looking down I saw an incoming video call from the conglomerate's chief of police. His profile picture was a professional photograph dressed in his most formal blues.

I accepted the call without turning the video on, I'd taken off my ridiculous coat and peacock shirt and was in an unflattering, but comfortable, white undershirt.

On the small screen of the hand terminal, the chief sat in his office, clean-shaven and wearing a colorful shirt and robe-like overcoat.

"Mr. Rungson I'm calling you to preemptively apologize for Detective Pikowski's report," Chief Stone said, he sounded flustered and spoke faster than seemed appropriate. "I'm aware that you're receiving files related to your father's death as they're being uploaded. And I wanted to let you know that after reviewing Pikowski's report I've decided to take her off the case and assign a more experienced and level-headed detective to your father's case."

"I haven't read the report yet," I said. "But I assume she accused me of being her prime suspect just like she did this morning." At the time I was shocked she said it to my face, but even more surprising was that she'd put it on an official document.

"She did. And I'm sorry for her behavior this morning. I'll make sure to take official disciplinary action for that wild accusation. I'm aware that there is plenty of documentation of your travels from Feldman's station this morning and that it is impossible and insulting to—"

"Keep her on," I said, then chuckled at the wide-eyed shock on the chief's face. I pulled up Pikowski's report on the large TV screen and scanned it. "Says here she wants to question me next?"

"Of course. But we're taking your father's death seriously. We're committed to finding his killer and will do whatever's necessary to bring him to justice."

I didn't share his confidence. As capable as Rungson police are there aren't any that can travel through the multiverse, at least not to my knowledge.

"Send Pikowski back over," I said. "I'll answer any questions she has. I want someone working on this case who isn't willing to overlook the impossible."

The chief agreed, had no choice to do anything else, but he couldn't hide the shocked and confused expression on his face.

I hung up before he shared any more niceties about my "father."

3

Detective Pikowski sat in the large white armchair across from the couch that I was seated on. She still wore the practical vest and long-sleeved collared shirt that she had on this morning. She seemed incapable or unwilling to get comfortable in the large seat, likely due to the badge, gun, and other tools strapped to her belt.

I'd put on a dark blue and slightly less chaotically patterned shirt over my undershirt to prepare for her arrival, but I didn't go as far as to button it up. I wanted to be presentable but also comfortable. After all, I was supposed to be a mourning heir, some dishevelment was acceptable.

The television to Pikowski's left had a few files related to my murder displayed. And she had a few more on the hand terminal in her lap. The same terminal that was recording our conversation.

She'd already asked me a dozen questions, all related to my travels from Feldman's station. I answered them as best I could, but considering that the paperwork was faked and I hadn't actually left Feldman's it was difficult to keep my story straight.

The only thing more uncomfortable than the melted and assaulted snowman statue was the fact that Pikowski knew I was lying but wasn't bold enough to accuse me of it. Likely due to a stern lecture from Chief Stone.

"And you arrived on the orbital satellite via high-speed gate transfer at 3:19?" Pikowski asked, for the third time.

"If that's what the documents say then it's true. I didn't pay too much attention to the time. Other things on my mind." I gestured at the screen on the wall.

"But transmissions related to your father's death didn't go out until 6:57. Were you aware of your father's death before the first public transmission."

"One would hope that the leaders of the conglomerate are at least a little more informed than the public," I said with a smile.

"So at 3:28 Griffith local time, you boarded the orbital entry shuttle landing you at the planet-side dockyards at 4:13?" Pikowski continued jumping back in the timeline to catch me off guard. "That's a tight turnaround."

"If this is just going to be questions about my itinerary I can direct you to my lawyers who are as familiar with the paperwork's timeline as you are." I groaned a little regretful that I'd agreed to this interrogation.

"Look, Monika," I said using her first name to attempt to be encouraging and familiar. "Ask me something interesting. About my father. About me. About what kind of conspiracy we're committing that might motivate someone to kill me." I wanted something to prove that she was the right detective for this strange case.

She looked at me while she chewed on the inside of her cheek contemplatively.

"Fine," she relented. "I've got something for you." She gestured at the TV. "May I?"

I gave her hand terminal control of the screen and smiled. Whatever she was about to show me had not been filed in the official records yet.

Pikowski stood up and walked to the side of the couch I was seated on. From her hand terminal, she transmitted a security video of the orbital satellite I was on this morning to the screen.

A crowd of people exited from the docking terminal and dispersed into the crowd. Facial recognition identified a few people automatically. Other than that it was an uninteresting video.

I shrugged.

She restarted the video but paused it before the doors opened and the crowd spilled out. "This is the high-speed gate transfer that arrived at 3:19. Point out to me where you are in that crowd?" She played the video.

I didn't bother watching it a second time. I looked at her, who was waiting and watching me.

"What else do you have?" I asked with a smile.

"I have footage of you boarding the orbital entry shuttle," she said. "And I have footage of you arriving on the orbital satellite."

"Good," I said. "Show me that one."

A little confused by my enthusiasm she played the security footage. Public satellite hubs like that are littered with security cameras and monitoring devices. Data was stored about every square inch of the place.

Pikowski played a video in the back hallway of the main path of foot traffic. Not too much was happening. Until I suddenly appeared out of nowhere.

It was the unmistakable scruffy-faced leather jacket and heavy boot wearing body that I traveled in. The only thing that followed me from universe to universe, when I wasn't taking over the body of a pre-existing Todd.

I could've appeared in a bathroom if I didn't want to be noticed. But there were cybertons of data and it would take a highly motivated person to spot me appearing in these corridors, let alone care about my mysterious appearance. And someone that motivated would easily notice that I hadn't ever walked into the bathroom. That kind of motivation was exactly what I needed if I was going to catch my killer.

"Care to explain how the same editing trick was applied to Rungson orbital satellite security footage as your father's house?" Pikowski said after a minute.

I was glad that I had someone so motivated working on this case. Now it was just a matter of directing her down the right path.

I stood up. I shrugged off my dark blue shirt, I liked it since it was less ridiculous than the rest of my wardrobe. I didn't want it to disappear.

The empty mug from this morning sat on the coffee table and I picked it up. I held it over the couch, uninterested in cleaning up the shattered mess since housekeeping would be gone for the rest of the week mourning my death.

"Turn off your recording," I told Pikowski. Before she protested I added, "If you upload anything I'm about to show you I'll just take it down. We both know I'm powerful enough to make it happen. Save us both the chaos."

She pressed some buttons on her hand terminal, but I couldn't be certain she'd ended her recording. And at a certain point, I was just going to have to trust her.

I took a deep breath reached out in my mind for a point a little further down on the frayed strand that was this timeline and exhaled.

My shoulders were instantly weighed down by my heavy leather duster.

Pikowski had moved to behind the white couch and she was pacing back and forth. Startled at my sudden appearance from her perspective she reached for the gun that rested on her hip.

I put my arms up in surrender uninterested in being killed a second time today.

While she caught her breath from my sudden arrival I shrugged off my leather duster to the couch over the coffee mug that had fallen there in my departure.

My cheeks were scruffy again, and the fact I'd have to shave twice in one day to maintain this universe's style was a little frustrating. But the black T-shirt and jeans that I was suddenly wearing were comfortable enough.

I took a relaxed seat on the armchair looking past the couch at Pikowski who was gathering words.

"You disappeared for like five minutes," she finally said, voice wavering as if she didn't know her statement was real. "Where did you go?"

"Nowhere," I said with a shrug. "I just jumped to this moment in time."

"You want me to believe you can travel through time?"

"Believe? You watched me do it," I said. "This requires as much faith as gravity. But let's look at the bigger picture."

"What bigger picture?" she asked sarcastically. "I need an explanation for what just happened here and now, in this room."

I didn't have one for her, at least not one that would appease her. I took control of the television again and replayed my murder. The killer disappeared after a deep breath, the kitchen knife dropped the the ground with a clatter.

Pikowski's eyes widened with shock.

"You did it!" she said. "You killed your father." Her hand rested on her gun the other hand reached for her handcuffs.

I shook my head still relaxed in the armchair. "I didn't kill anyone this morning. I was the one laying in that bed."

The detective looked from me to her hand terminal. "The resemblance *is* uncanny."

"DNA records will confirm I'm the same as well," I said. "Someone digs it up every few decades, but truth be told no one's super interested in conspiracies about their conglomerate leader being a clone or a time traveler or an alien being."

"What the hell am I supposed to do with this then?" Pikowski asked.

"Same thing you were doing this morning. Find my killer. Except now you actually have all the information."

"How am I supposed to track down a time traveler?" She asked.

It was a good question. One I had asked myself a few times.

Up to this point, I just wanted to have someone to share the mystery with. But Pikowski had already proved to be a better detective than I ever was in any of my past lives. And tracking down a killer capable of traveling the multiverse would need someone remarkably talented.

4

As far as space stations went Gretchen didn't think this was a bad one to be stranded on. Not that she'd visited many space stations. She preferred to stick to contemporary timelines, or at least timelines that were contemporary to her.

When she'd worked for Woah Te and the rest of the avians of the Mother Tree she'd seen a lot of different versions of her Earth and humanity. All of them on the cusp of various technological revolutions.

It was fun. It was familiar. It was comfortable.

Almost as comfortable as this space station's spa. Which had everything she could imagine she wanted, and then some. Machines to massage you. Showers with exact temperatures, which were almost useless to her because she was unfamiliar with Celsius.

Her favorite was the bathtubs that automatically dispensed bubbles, herbs, and salts. It even maintained the temperature of the bath water as you bathed to avoid having to refill it or get out before you wanted to. And she didn't get out earlier than she wanted to.

But now she was pruney and relaxed and ready to see the rest of the space station. Todd hadn't returned or sent her a change of clothes. She wrapped her hair in a towel and pulled on her familiar traveling clothes, a blue T-shirt, and some jeans. Practical, useful, and fashionable enough in the timelines she liked to visit.

She left the black leather coat and tennis shoes in the spa, they'd followed her around the multiverse, she wasn't likely to lose them in a hermetically sealed space station.

One thing she was not going to forget was her grandmother's gold wristwatch. Well not exactly *her* grandmother, but close enough. Its shattered face wasn't very effective at telling time anymore. But ironically, as a time traveler, she didn't need the information often.

She clasped the watch around her left wrist using her right hand. The striking purple tattoo on her right wrist was dormant for now, and she hoped the nitthog would stay that way for a while. The watch hung loose and comfortable on her wrist, just tight enough to not slip past her hand.

"Computer," she spoke into thin air and her voice echoed around the metal walls of the spa. The whole station had a clean and crisp feel, like a hospital or brand-new office building. She was used to places with history, grime, character.

"Yes Mrs. Smith," the computer responded, and it sounded almost as if a real person spoke through the station's speakers. The computer had a masculine voice and an accent that was hard to place. It sounded proper like she'd expect an old-timey butler to have.

Todd's preferences were likely a product of his time, and in at least this way Gretchen could relate to him.

But sometimes it felt like that was the only way she could relate to him. Despite them being the only humans they knew that could travel through the multiverse. This Todd was cold, secretive, and independent to the point of seeming disconnected from reality.

Guess she would be too if she had been untethered from her memories like him. Instead, she could remember everything she'd ever done. An ability nearly as remarkable as being able to travel through the multiverse. Every life she lived, every action she took, all in her head like a movie.

She even remembered the many jobs she'd done for the avians. As much as she wanted to forget those. They still rose up.

But she'd had long lives between them that she could focus on instead.

"I'd like a tour of the station," Gretchen told the computer.

"Very well," the computer responded then directed her through the hallways of the space station.

The computer seemed as intricately wired to the satellite as the artificial gravity system that kept her water in the bathtub and her bare feet on the cold metal floor. It was remarkable, more advanced than all the technology she'd experienced in her lifetimes on Earth and humanity's expansion of technology.

There was so much she'd never get used to on this ship.

The computer led her to the gym. It had a court with vinyl flooring. She knew it'd be strange to see the maple floors she was used to playing on in such a futuristic ship, but she still couldn't help but think of it as cheap, despite the ship's other amenities. There was a room with countless weights and weight machines and a running track that looped above it all.

The computer informed her that robots could be called up to play basketball, volleyball, or sonicball with her if she was interested. After a relaxing bath, she was not, but she kept it in mind for later.

She didn't know how long she'd be stuck on this satellite. She hoped it wouldn't be long. But she was glad there'd be something for her to do for fun.

Gretchen hoped Todd would be back soon. She'd expected him back almost instantaneously. It was the natural thing to do considering he could time travel. But he hadn't returned despite the ages she'd spent in the bath.

The computer showed her a kitchen, a spacious room with multiple stoves and ovens. It was more similar to a restaurant kitchen than a household kitchen.

Passing through the kitchen there was a massive ballroom which explained the kitchen's size. It was filled with cloth-covered tables, white chairs, and a dance floor in the center.

A bar at the far end of the ballroom had countless bottles of alcohol behind it on the shelves. Although the shelves did have a few empty slots where the bottles had been taken but not replaced.

The computer offered to make her a drink, detecting her interest by her prolonged study of the ballroom's bar. But she declined for now. It felt like it was midmorning to her.

The ballroom connected to a casino. Bright neon lights that flashed in rainbow colors filled the room. The floor was a colorful and chaotic pattern that made her think of old skating rinks. Styles were cyclical after all.

There were felt-covered tables for every kind of game you could bet on, a few of which she didn't recognize. Slot machines, some digital some mechanical, created a maze that she had to navigate through. Jazzy music played in the background and this room felt alive, even if no one was in it.

Gretchen couldn't imagine who Todd might gamble against. But he had said he didn't use most of the rooms in this place. And the thin plastic film over some of the slot machines made that clear.

The casino exited on the outermost ring of the space station. This hallway was familiar to her. She could look out the large overarching glass windows and see all the stars. Jupiter wasn't in view from this end of the satellite but she knew they orbited the gas giant.

Gretchen didn't like looking into the black expanse of space. It reminded her too much of those existential nights in college where she could feel the whole multiverse around her and how small she was in it.

Thick metal airlocks the size of garage doors lined the walls. Spaceships could dock into them, there was a red one somewhere around the ring with a strange machine inside of it. As fun as it had been to float in the thing as Todd unpacked the equipment he'd sent himself, she wasn't eager to go back as the beating purple heart was creepy.

After a walk around about sixty degrees of the outer circle a corridor led back to the central hub of the station. The hallway was lined with doors sized for humans, not cargo.

She peaked her head in a few of them as she made it down the hallway. They were all identical. A small sitting area with a couch and small kitchen-like counter, with a device the size and shape of a microwave on it.

A pocket door inside the room led to a bedroom with a king-size bed and desk. An en suite bathroom was connected to the bedroom, small and compact but still reasonably comfortable. They lacked a bathtub but who needed one when there was a spa across the station?

When Gretchen got to a particular door the computer notified her that it was the room that Todd used. There was no security in the station, which hadn't seemed prudent to Todd considering he planned to live here alone, but she left him his privacy anyway.

How strange this Todd was compared to the one she grew up with—grew old with. Her Todd had been anxious and stayed away from others because of it. This Todd, he seemed to be alone because he thought so little of the rest of the world.

But why build a space station that looked like a hotel if you were just going to live in it alone? Gretchen didn't see why he hadn't spent the money on something more personalized, not like he had a shortage of it. And she'd seen, ages ago when he took her to his life with Gretchen, that he was capable of filling a house with sentimental memories.

She couldn't fathom having enough money to build something this big. She couldn't fathom the entirety of humanity having enough money or technology to pull this off, let alone one man. She felt like a Neanderthal looking at a flip phone.

"Mrs. Smith," the computer said in its charming male voice, "you've received a message at the central terminal."

She made her way to the central chamber. Now that she'd seen two of the station's six hallways she could tell where this central area had been remodeled to fit Todd's taste.

It had a sunken in seating area with a bar around it. At one far edge, there was a wall of monitors and a high-backed swivel chair.

If this was supposed to be the main hub for people to pass through to other arms of the station it should've had more places to meet up, chat, and direct people where they needed to go. It should've looked like a hotel lobby.

But instead, Todd had stripped it of anything useful that might acknowledge that others were supposed to be there. She could see the bolt-holes where seating and tables could be installed. She could see the colorful pathways on the ground meant to direct traffic around those seating areas.

Instead of all that Todd put a massive computer and a few bars that would automatically mix and deliver drinks. Obviously to help him ignore the rest of the vacant station.

The room made Gretchen feel empty and lonely in a way that having the spa to herself didn't.

Gretchen took a seat in the high-backed chair. A dozen monitors looked down on her. Most were security feeds of empty rooms in the station. Other screens logged vital functions of the station with graphs and numbers that Gretchen didn't care to take the time to comprehend.

The desk in front of the chair had a few monitors embedded in it and a thumb-sized rectangular piece of plastic. Todd had called it a USB. If there was anything Gretchen'd learned about traveling to different contemporary universes it was that they all approached technology a little differently.

So this piece of plastic begged the question, why does it exist in a world where it couldn't be read or manufactured?

The computer directed her gaze to the central terminal in front of her face, the obvious place to put your focus if you weren't so stunned by the copious technology around you.

Text appeared on the screen. Gretchen was a little shocked. She'd expected a video, a hologram, anything more advanced than email.

Mrs. Smith,

Todd requested that I send the attached information related to a USB thumb drive along with a shipment of clothing. Since it's clear now he was true to his word and didn't return to Griffith I feel it is my turn to fulfill my end of the bargain.

As I understand it the Fortress computer should be able to manufacture and program a converter without much input from you.

Once that's completed I urge you to read the drive immediately and take action on whatever information it contains. My sources here believed that the machine delivered is critical to Todd's escape from a looming threat.

I'm proud of the work the members of his conglomerate have achieved in his absence. However, as I creep towards the end of a second century and understand the burden of leadership better I realize I may have been too harsh on him. If and when you see him again, let him know this for me. And maybe encourage him to visit an old friend before it's too late. If it's ever too late for a time traveler like him.

From Times Past,

Monika Pikowski

The message left Gretchen with more questions than answers. This Monika person couldn't travel but was familiar with their abilities. Todd had said he'd return but hadn't, a feeling she was beginning to relate to.

And worst of all she didn't look forward to dealing with the creepy purple-hearted contraption on her own.

"Should I begin manufacturing the converter as Mrs. Pikowski suggested?" the computer asked.

Gretchen took a deep breath. She wished she could disappear, but that would bring an army of avians in tow. She exhaled and stayed in her seat.

"Let's see what's on this thing," Gretchen said, more confident than she felt.

5

I sat on the couch sipping on a glass of whiskey, or at least what passed for whiskey on Griffith. The drink mostly consisted of a variant of corn, with enough rye in there to fool the locals into thinking it was nice.

I could have off-world stuff shipped in, but the nicest stuff in Central System would still taste like cheap imitation to me. And right now I didn't feel like making a trip to Scotland, Ireland, or Kentucky for the real stuff.

The cup in my hand was thick crystal glass with ridges around the outside. Its matching decanter sat on the marble coffee table a quarter full of brown liquor. I rubbed my finger over the glass's ridges thinking about who'd killed me and why.

And most importantly if they'd do it again.

I had a bright yellow stun gun resting next to the decanter just in case they tried. It had a single shot. I should've had more guns but they were hard to get my hands on in a pinch. I'd borrowed this one from Detective Pikowski before she left.

I had a few other, more deadly, weapons stashed around the room and house as a whole. I wasn't afraid for my life I just didn't want the killer to escape if they ever returned.

My mouth tasted like the savory fried rice I'd ordered for dinner. Just because Linda was gone didn't mean that I'd have to settle for something rehydrated in the foodcrowave. The takeout container, thin plastic, was still sitting on the table with its single-use utensils inside.

"Who wanted me dead?" I asked myself. Likely plenty of people considering my blunt personality. But not many of them could chase me through the multiverse.

If I could figure out who it was I could figure out why. But I couldn't go scouring the multiverse for them. The place was too big for that. Meaning they'd have to come to me.

I didn't love being the bait. But I didn't have any better ideas.

So I waited here, in the living room, with a whiskey and a stun gun, listening for the sound of rubber sneakers on the tile floor of my kitchen.

As time passed I kicked my bare feet kicked up on the coffee table and got comfortable. I almost didn't expect them to show.

By the time I heard the footsteps, they were in the same room as me.

I reached for the stun gun. The thick leather belt around my neck pulled me into the thick white cushions of the couch.

The killer pulled the belt up into my jaw. It'd crush my windpipe if they kept it up.

With the whiskey glass in my hand I beat against the killer's hands that held the belt in place. It was not persuasive enough.

I reached higher and slammed the glass against their hooded head. The glass shattered in my hand and the killer stumbled back.

My neck was free of their belt and I reached for the stun gun on the table.

The killer, wearing all black just like before, lurched over the couch and at me.

I fired the gun. The metal probes leaped out of the barrel. A high-frequency buzz was the only sound that followed.

The prongs embedded themselves in the attacker's shoulder and chest but the thick material of their hooded jacket protected him from the full force of the shock.

They tackled me into the coffee table. My back hit the glass whiskey decanter uncomfortably. It fell off the table. Shattered on the ground.

The rest of me hit the marble slab of the table which didn't feel much better.

The killer was shorter than me. Their face was still covered by a bandana, but their irises were ice blue. The corners of the eyes had wrinkles around them along with the part of their forehead that wasn't covered by the ball cap.

I pushed them off me as they reached for my throat. They landed between the couch and the ugly snowman statue.

I got to my feet as fast as I could. Flipped the coffee table over so it lay on its side under the TV screen. I'd taped a hunting knife to the bottom of the table. It was an antique gifted to me by some conglomerate head ages ago. It'd never been used, and for that reason, it was shockingly sharp.

I pulled it out of the sheath which stayed taped to the table and brandished it at the killer. At some point in time, I'd likely been trained to use a knife. But I'd forgotten that life like many others. Right now I wished I had the infallible memory Gretchen spoke of.

The killer put his fists up and approached me in a sideways stance. His right leg, the bad one, was forward.

Once he was within reach I slashed at him with the knife. The killer blocked it with their arm but the sharp blade cut through their clothes and flesh with ease. The knife's edge was red with blood.

The killer's fist connected with my mouth while my hands were wide. The punch was strong enough to knock a tooth loose.

Stunned for a minute the killer hit my arm that held the knife. Grabbing my fingers they were able to pry the weapon from my hand.

Unwilling to give the killer the upper hand I kicked their bad leg out from under them.

As the killer fell they buried the knife in my thigh.

I howled in pain. Putting weight on the leg was nearly impossible and dark red blood flowed out of the wound and onto my jeans.

The killer lay back on the ground in front of the TV. The coffee table loomed over them, turned on its side.

I saw the killer's chest rise and fall. It wasn't the labored breath of exhaustion. It was a calm focused breath.

I took a painful step towards them. Gripped the edge of the coffee table with both hands.

I slammed the marble table onto their chest.

The weight of the table ended their breathing. This body was dead, but the killer lived on, somewhere in the expansive multiverse.

I fell back on the ground unable to hold myself up with my leg anymore. I leaned against the bottom of the bloody white couch.

By killing them I'd let them escape.

But at least now I had a body.

6

Monika Pikowski sat behind her desk at the station. It'd been a long day, everyone else had headed home. She was left typing up a report summarizing her interrogation of Mr. Todd Rungson V. Although the number behind the name, according to Mr. Rungson, delineated nothing.

The office was nearly empty. She'd unbuttoned the tight vest she'd worn all day. Her badge and gun rested in her desk drawer no longer digging into her hip. At least her flats were comfortable enough.

Every movement she made echoed off the concrete walls of the building. The tall polished sheet metal that separated the detectives' workstations began to reflect the city's skyline that came in from the large window.

The central police station she worked at was downtown. She didn't mind delaying her commute and skipping rush hour. Kot could take care of dinner himself.

She needed a quiet place to think and a crowded subway car was not conducive to that. An empty office on the other hand, perfect.

And Monika needed to think because she couldn't believe what she'd just gotten herself into.

Her mother always said her big mouth would get her into trouble. Not that the criticism ever kept Monika quiet.

Accusing the conglomerate head of patricide, to his face no less, was one thing. Putting the accusation in her official report was another.

She didn't care. She was going to do what was right. Even if it cost her her dream job.

And it almost had. Except her main suspect vouched for her, and forced the chief to keep her on the case.

Chief Stone was clearly bitter about it. She knew taking on the murder of a conglomerate head would change her career trajectory, but she didn't expect it to change like this.

But her future career was the least of her problems.

In the nicest house she'd ever visited, Mr. Rungson revealed he could, allegedly, travel through time.

No, not just time, through the multiverse. That seemed to be an important distinction to him.

She was still hesitant to believe it. Along with the long explanation of his powers he'd given her afterward.

He thought it was critical to the case. She thought it was evidence enough to get him checked into a long-term psychiatric hospital.

But for now, she was taking him at his word, even if it was clear he wasn't telling her everything. She didn't have anything to prove he was lying, aside from the ridiculousness of his claims. But she learned the hard way that ridiculous wasn't the same as a lie.

She'd verified the DNA. He was in fact identical to his father, grandfather, and all his forefathers. The info was right there in the open for countless people to see, just like the security footage of the orbital satellite.

But most people didn't want to solve mysteries. Most people didn't want to see the truth, even if it was in front of their eyes. Monika hated leaving things in the dark.

However, she didn't know what she was supposed to do about the case in front of her.

Half of the digital forensic team was banging their head against the wall trying to prove the security footage was edited, the other half was trying to run facial recognition on a sliver of a face. A face which, according to Mr. Rungson, likely wasn't born in this universe, and therefore unregistered on all the forensic databases.

Monika couldn't question people with motives. She couldn't review travel logs and documentation. She couldn't check alibis considering the murderer could travel through time!

She had squat for leads. Rungson didn't have much more. And he knew it. It's why he roped her into this.

Chief Stone didn't put her on this case by accident. He put her on the case because he knew she'd get to the bottom of it when other detectives would give up or phone it in. She'd done it before, she'll do it again.

But how was she going to do it on this case? She felt so small and helpless.

She submitted the half-assed interrogation report. Rungson wouldn't complain, he didn't want half the stuff he told her documented anyway. And if Chief Stone complained, well he'd have to take it up with his boss, Rungson.

Then she pulled out some dry-erase markers from her desk drawer. The other reason she thought it best to stay and wait for there to be no one around. A dozen different software systems claimed they could help her capture her thoughts better than a dry-erase marker on polished sheet metal. But for Monika, they all fell short.

She wrote out what she knew. Which wasn't much.

First, she knew the killer appeared in a hood and face mask, meaning this was pre-meditated.

Second, did the killer know Rungson could travel? If so they knew killing him wouldn't keep him dead. If not, then this was revenge against a conglomerate head. A pitty when you could jump to a multiverse and put yourself in charge like Rungson did.

Third, and most shocking, the killer had gone above and beyond. The gash on Rungson IV's throat was deep, thorough, effective. And so were the 11 stabbings.

The thoroughness combined with Rungson's immortality felt like the killer was making a threat. It felt like the killer was making a point.

But threats came with demand. Came with desires. If Rungson knew who the threat was coming from he didn't need to get Monika involved.

He was a conglomerate head. There were plenty of powerful people that would benefit from him disappearing. This morning she had expected that to be the direction this case went. It's why she suspected Todd Rungson V.

But if Rungson could travel the multiverse he was more powerful than she could imagine, and likely made more enemies than she could imagine. Especially since Rungson knew he could disappear without a trace after wronging them.

She put most of this on the metal wall in shorthand using a red marker. Her handwriting was made of sharp lines that were nearly illegible, a consequence of constantly using computer terminals, but it was good enough for her.

She made a few more markings before her hand terminal interrupted her thought process. She tried to remember if she'd scheduled something tonight. Had she told her mother she'd be over for dinner?

Had Kot, remarkably, called her? Was there another obligation she'd forgotten?

She looked at her hand terminal and saw the portrait of Mr. Rungson who was video-calling her. She straightened her unbuttoned vest as best she could and made sure the collar of her shirt was even before answering.

Rungson looked like he'd fallen into a recycler and come out the other end. He was missing a tooth, his face was covered in wet blood and his long hair was disheveled, more so than usual.

The white leather couch behind him was also splattered with red blood that stood out like a cop in a strip club.

"Elder's light!" Monika said. The curse came out before she could compose herself. "Are you okay?"

He smiled in a way that no one in his state should be smiling. "Not particularly. But I have good news."

She found that hard to believe. "What is that?"

He switched cameras to show the room around him. The living room she'd just questioned Mr. Rungson in was covered in blood and shattered glass.

The marble coffee table was pushed against the wall and off-kilter.

It was off-kilter because a person in all black had been crushed under it.

"I caught our killer," he said. He sounded like a schoolboy who'd just gotten his first kiss from a girl.

The change in perspective also showed a thick wooden handled knife buried deep in Rungson's thigh. His rugged blue pants were covered in dark red blood.

"You're bleeding!" Monika said, "I'll send an ambulance over immediately."

"No," Rungson said.

If he wasn't her boss's boss's boss she would've ignored him.

He switched the camera to show his stupid grin again, although this time she could see a grimace working its way in from the edges.

"Don't send anyone," he said. "Just come over by yourself."

"Bleeding that much you'll die before I can—" She cut herself off once she figured it out.

Rungson's devious grin reached his eyes. It was clear messing with people like this was a pastime.

She was not a fan.

7

In a body that was unmarred and jeans and a T-shirt that weren't covered in blood, I led Pikowski into the living room. My boots thudded on the ground as we walked through the house.

Even to the most seasoned cop, it must've been strange to see my body lying in front of the couch in a pool of blood while I stood next to her looking nearly identical.

But Detective Pikowski was a professional. If the tightly button vest she wore hadn't given it away her immediate reaction would've.

She didn't gasp in horror at the two dead bodies, nor did she start poking around. She pulled some rubber gloves out of a crime scene inspection bag and slipped them on carefully.

I hadn't touched anything in the room since the scuffle. Once my leg let out enough blood that I died I appeared in a much neater version of this white living room, the same melted and assaulted snowman statue in the corner.

I returned with a breath to this universe, my traveling clothes once again on me. If I ever needed a quick buck I could sell an infinite supply of genuine leather dusters. Right now two of them were piled unceremoniously behind the bloody couch.

If Pikowski had any discomfort or shock she hid it well. She kept looking from me to the identical body on the floor. She studied our matching features like it was yet another clue in this mystery.

If she didn't believe me at lunch, she'd have to believe me now.

With a dozen evidence baggies in her hand, Pikowski began her work. I explained the fight, the loose belt, discharged taser, and bloody knife, as she worked. She listened quietly, labeling bags as needed.

I wanted to ask for the knife back, it was worth at least as much as the hover car she'd driven here in, but it felt unprofessional to get in the way of her work.

She meticulously inspected my dead body. She took pictures of it, along with the rest of the living room. It was a slow process, but I was tired and unwilling to get in her way. It's why I kept her on the case.

Finally, we got to the body of the killer. She needed help lifting the marble coffee table off of the body. I was shocked that I'd been able to flip the thing in the heat of the fight.

We leaned it against the wall, under the TV screen, and Monika took thorough pictures of the body and the table. The process was slow and I was eager to get to unmasking the figure on the ground.

If I knew them I'd know where to find them. If I didn't... well I hope it didn't come to that.

Pikowski recorded the killer was 1.75 meters tall a number that should've meant something to me considering how much time I'd spent in the future. To me, they looked just under average height.

After what felt like forever Detective Pikowski carefully pulled the killer's hood back and lifted off their baseball hat.

The man was bald on the top of his head but had thick white hair above his ears and the back of his neck. He looked like an old-timey monk but I knew he just lived in a time period where they unfortunately didn't have a great solution for hair loss.

Pikowski lowered the bandanna revealing a bulbous nose and a thick white mustache. There were some wrinkles around his cheeks and under his lips.

I was a little disappointed that I'd been beaten up by someone so old. Sure I could technically have lived a longer life. But my body, an apparent mid-thirties, should've been spry enough to take him on.

"Do you know him?" Pikowski asked.

I looked at his icy blue eyes, glassy with death, and tried to think through all the old men I knew. Some were mentors, some were frustrating bureaucrats. A few were conglomerate heads who'd seen the rise and fall of civilizations.

"I don't recognize him," I said. Frustrated that our lead had failed to deliver.

Pikowski began rummaging through his pockets. I didn't expect her to find anything. I couldn't bring items with me through the multiverse. Any clothes I wore when traveling disappeared and I always appeared in the same outfit.

The front pockets of the black jeans the killer wore were empty, they were tight enough that it'd be difficult to conceal anything. The killer's hooded jacket had a large kangaroo pocket on the front.

Pikowski reached her gloved hand in and brought out a quartz-like crystal hanging from a black cord. It looked like a necklace. It wasn't truly quarts since it wasn't the familiar milky white. Instead, this thing seemed clear and filled with a thick white mist that fogged up the interior.

The mist seemed to give off an imperceptible glow. I turned off the room's light using a voice command. All that was illuminated was the detective's frustrated face.

"Turn them back on please," she said, in a strained and reserved voice. I got the feeling I was only moments away from receiving a scolding in her cop voice, and if it hadn't been for my status as a conglomerate head she would've gotten it out already.

She dropped the crystal in an evidence bag. I reached my hand out to inspect it. She ignored the gesture and wrote a case number on it with a black permanent marker.

"You said you couldn't travel with items," Pikowski said. The question was an innocent enough interrogation. She probably didn't even notice she was doing it.

"I can't," I said. I gestured at the belt, looped tightly in another plastic bag on the floor. "But if you're wearing something it travels with you."

"Why take this off then?" She asked.

"Didn't want to give me an offensive edge," I said casually. It seemed a simple enough explanation. Although the cord the crystal hung from looked like it'd snap before choking anyone out.

"You ever see a rock like this?" Pikowski asked.

I reached out for the bag to examine it closer. She gave it to me, reluctantly. The cord looked like it was a natural material woven together. I thought of it as jute twine but it could belong to a plant native to any of the millions of planets in the stars.

A silver metal wire was wrapped around one end of the crystal. The whole rock had flat edges and came to a tip like the yellow pencils I used in school.

I opened the baggy. The zip-top let out a snap. It gave me away.

"Keep that sealed," Pikowski said. I hadn't been talked to with that much firmness in this world for literally generations.

I pulled the crystal out by the necklace cord anyway.

Pikowski marched up to me leaving the crushed body of the killer behind.

"You think this is some kind of game?" Pikowski asked. "You were murdered less than an hour ago."

The mist inside the crystal seemed to be obscuring something. I reached out to pull it closer to my face.

Pikowski's blue gloved hand wrapped around my wrist to keep me from grabbing it. Her effort was half-hearted or underestimated how little I cared about procedure. I'd brought her on for a second point of view, not bureaucratic nonsense.

The crystal landed in my hand. I felt the zap of an electric shock when it landed. I wanted to let go of it in response but the stone seemed welded to my hand.

From the edges of my vision static began to creep in. I looked around the room expecting to spot a void figure, the lanky black humanoids that trailed this visual anomaly.

The void figure obscured the form of whatever traveler was looking into this universe. Gretchen had done it to me. The avians we'd escaped from could do it too.

But none of them should've known where I was. Although I would've said the same about the balding killer as well.

Pikowski's grip on my wrist tightened. But she wasn't trying to pull me away from the crystal anymore. It was like she was hanging on to me.

I looked at her as the static crept in from the edges of my vision. Her dark brown eyes were wide in shock. They darted around in confusion trying to take in what she was seeing.

I expected the static to swallow her up like it swallowed up the couch, the statue, and the dead body. But her face stayed clear to me only a few feet away.

Then the floor dropped out from under us and we were falling into the static grey void.

8

Pikowski and I stood at the edge of a gleaming white room. The floor, walls, and ceiling were a dazzling pearlescent. Hints of pink and purple shone on the surface of the creamy white material.

As beautiful as it was it was eerie how silent the room was. Any sound we made echoed through the dazzling and cavernous room.

The whole room smelled of salt water and a fish market. It wasn't unpleasant, but I wouldn't be buying a scented candle of the smell anytime soon. It reminded me of eating sushi, gutting catfish, and trawling for orange kingfish on Ortho IV lifetimes ago.

It was only a marginal improvement on the wooden library that the avians dropped me in. And I didn't like being forced across the multiverse, or out of it, against my will. I didn't like that I'd fallen for a trap.

I especially didn't like that I'd fallen for a trap Pikowski had warned me about.

The floor had a domed pattern running along it. Like a mole had dug under it and displaced the ground just enough to be noticeable but not enough to trip anyone up.

My long leather jacket hung on my shoulders, the rest of my clothes were the familiar t-shirt and jeans I traveled in. The necklace was no longer in my hand.

If I'd been wearing it, would it have traveled with me? I wondered.

Pikowski wore her vest, collared button-up shirt, slacks, and comfortable flats. Her police officer utility belt was still wrapped around her waist, her gun, handcuffs, and badge strapped to it. Thin blue gloves were still on her hands as she let go of my wrist.

I thought some of what she wore might be useful, now or in the future if she wound up traveling again. Although I certainly didn't want to make a habit of dragging her, or anyone else, through the multiverse.

I was responsible for dragging Gretchen into this. I wouldn't burden anyone else with the curse.

Based on the sickly green color of Pikowski's face she didn't want to make a habit of it either. She looked away from me and doubled over leaning against the pearlescent wall we stood near.

She held back her short black hair but didn't hurl. After a few coughs, some hard swallows, and a couple of deep breaths she stood at attention looking at me.

Her gaze was ferocious like a lion that'd just figured out the cage door was open.

"What in the name of the Holy Elders was that?" Pikowski spat at me.

"I'm as clue—"

"I told you not to touch that thing," she continued. "You think I wasn't curious? You don't trust me? I'd accuse you of wanting me fired but now I think you just want me to look incompetent."

"It's not—"

"You've got a maniac killing you. I've got a pissed-off boss looking to fire me. And you're telling me fairy stories about multidimensional travel. Except now I can't accuse you of being delusional because now you've roped me into it too."

I shrugged, no longer willing to get in the way of this train.

"I'd kick your ass if you weren't the most powerful person of Griffith. I'd arrest you if you weren't my only ticket out of here. I'd shoot you if you weren't immortal and hadn't been killed once today. Hell, maybe that's a good enough reason to do it anyway."

She didn't reach for her gun though. So I had that going for me.

"Where the hell are we?" she asked, sounding a little more calm. She pulled off her blue gloves and scratched at the wall with her fingernail.

When she didn't fire any more rants at me I answered.

"I don't know."

She let out an exasperated sigh. "Of course you don't. Can you get us out of here?"

I took a deep breath. Tried to find my bearings in the multiverse. Came up short.

I couldn't travel. It was like someone'd stolen my powers away again. I wasn't a fan of how easy that was to do.

"I can't get us out of here."

"Of course not," Pikowski replied sounding unsurprised and disappointed but at least she wasn't shouting anymore.

I looked at the ground. The dome lines that ran back and forth were about two inches high. There was one on each side giving us a pathway just narrow enough that Pikowski and I couldn't stand shoulder to shoulder.

I followed it a little and the pathway diverged left and right. I looked across the room it was difficult to see the other end of it even if nothing blocked my sightline.

"It's a maze," Pikowski said from behind me.

"Not a very effective one," I replied as I stepped over the small dome our first path T'd off in.

My boot immediately hit an invisible barrier. I cursed more out of shock than the pain.

"What?!?"

"Nothing," I said trying not to panic her. "There's an invisible wall."

Pikowski felt out carefully and slowly. Her hand stopped on the wall and she inspected it, as best she could, with her hands. She squatted down. Felt where it intersected the dome on the floor. She reached as high up as she could, pressed against it, then gave it a few kicks with the side of her foot.

I'd compare her to a mime but her inspection was more thorough than anything the striped comics could pull off.

"You any good at mazes?" I asked Pikowski once she seemed finished with her inspection.

"Not particularly," she replied with a frown.

"Me neither," I replied. "But I read somewhere that if you keep your right hand on the wall you'll eventually solve it. Something to do with the topology of the puzzle."

"Lead the way," she said resting her hands on her belt.

I put my right hand out and pressed it against the wall. It felt smooth and flimsy like a sheet hanging on a clothesline. But if I put any weight on it the wall pushed back becoming as ridged as concrete.

"You're taking this quite well," I said to Pikowski when we were about midway through the room.

We'd found a few dead ends so far but we just looped out of them by following my right-hand method. It was slow and frustrating but for all I knew I had all the time in the world. Pikowski on the other hand, well I hoped she had time as well.

"I'm sorry I lost it on you," she replied. "I try to avoid it, as a point but," it was clear it was hard for her to put what we were experiencing into words.

"All things considered I can't blame you."

"When you said you traveled the multiverse I figured you meant like go back in time, see old Earth, hang out with some Vikings, maybe check out early moon colonies."

"Vikings, in general, were assholes," I said. "And smelled like a broken recycler most days. I stick to periods post indoor plumbing, ideally post UBI if I can help it. Keeps me from having to scrounge for cash when I show up."

"You, scrounging for cash," Pikowski laughed. "I'd like to see it."

"You and about half the population of Griffith," I replied. "But to your original point, no, I don't typically travel anywhere as strange as this."

Pikowski laughed at that louder than I thought the comment deserved. Then under her breath, she said, "To our right, there's a figure."

"What about you do any traveling?" I asked loudly.

I raised my right hand which was tracing the wall at my waist up to my shoulder and looked past it. Sure enough on the opposite end of the room where we'd started a silhouette of a human, or human-shaped being, stood.

"I get around Griffith when I can. Try to stay close to home though. I've got family in the city."

"We get through this I'll get you a ticket to Feldman's. It's packed but a good time." I said it jovially as if it was completely normal to be cracking jokes in the middle of a pearlescent maze.

Not that I imagined anyone had a good gauge for what normal was in these scenarios.

As we slowly plodded through the maze it felt like we were backtracking more than making progress. The silhouette would appear and disappear. It wasn't particularly entertaining to solve the maze, I couldn't imagine it was entertaining to watch us. But I wasn't willing to waste time running through corridors and getting lost retracing paths I'd already been down.

Pikowski and I didn't say much to each other as we solved the maze. She likely didn't want to give anything away to whoever was watching us, sound carried in the room and the walls, while a hindrance for us, didn't seem to affect the sounds we made.

I didn't know what to say to her. It seemed too early to apologize since god knows how much more crap I was going to get her in before all this was over. And talking about politics, sports, or the weather seemed inconsequential considering I was in charge of two out of three of those things in Griffith.

Never was a fan of running sports teams...

The silhouette came into view clearer. It was a man. He wore black. But instead of a hoodie and a ball cap, he had a round bowler hat, a black suit, and slacks. The whole outfit was polished and pressed.

The face was familiar, wrinkled with ice-blue eyes and snow-white hair peeking out from under the hat. I was willing to bet he was bald under the hat.

It was my killer.

Frustratingly the maze guided us away from him we hit a dead end a few feet away from him. I glowered at him as we passed. He said nothing, just a simple, professional smile.

Patience was important as a killer.

I would know.

"What do you want to do?" Pikowski whispered after we had been dragged back towards the center of the maze and the killer no longer stood at the exit waiting for us.

"Hear him out," I said. "Maybe he wants to monologue."

Pikowski groaned but didn't suggest anything better.

"You can't arrest him," I pointed out, "Well you could, but I doubt it would get us far. If he wanted us dead he wouldn't have us waste time solving this maze."

"Unless he wants us worn out before facing us," Pikowski pointed out.

She was right. We'd been walking for a while. Neither of us was out of breath but the constant back and forth and thoroughness with which we covered the maze was a couple thousand steps.

We had to walk a few hundred more steps before it was over. I almost didn't realize it I was focused on keeping my hand against the wall.

Pikowski got my attention and I looked up. The pathway, lined with small half-cylinder borders, led straight to the suited killer. There were no ridges cutting through the path to diverge us forward. It was maybe half a football field from me to the killer.

I could sprint but I doubted I'd catch him off guard. I walked slowly, catching my breath, and filling my reserves of energy. Unsure what the man had planned for us next. Maybe an obstacle course. Maybe he'd force us to do a stack of crossword puzzles.

I stopped short of the maze's exit, keeping a half dozen yards between me and the killer. He was a capable fighter. I didn't want to get into a scrap with him on his home turf. Pikowski stood behind me, I didn't want to be responsible for anything worse happening to her.

"Congratulations," the killer said. He stood up straight, his arms behind his back pulling his chest tight in the well-fitted suit. His wrinkly mouth smiled and it almost seemed genuine.

"What do you want?" I asked.

"You're the one who came to me Todd," he said. His voice was silky smooth. It echoed through the room like we were in a concert hall. "But I don't see why you would bring a friend."

"I don't like being a lone wolf," I said.

"No," he said, "I suppose you don't. Part of how we got into this mess."

He moved subtly and before I could register what was going on deafening explosions came from behind me.

I leaned against the invisible wall. Pikowski had fired her handgun.

Her shots, while accurate, seemed to bounce off an invisible force-field around the killer.

But her attack wasn't unjustified. The killer had a gun of his own. This one was a little more bulbous and significantly less deafening.

A flash of red light, the sound of electricity through the air, and the smell of ozone were the only clues I had that the killer had fired something.

And it wasn't as benign as a stun gun.

I looked at Pikowski. The laser the killer had shot her with burned a fist-sized hole through the breast pocket of her faux leather vest.

Her face was frozen in a stunned expression. Her last thoughts were likely trying to figure out why her bullets hadn't landed.

A cauterized hole of singed black organs made a tunnel through her chest. On the other side, I could see the purple and pink sheens of the pearlescent ground.

There was no blood to taint it.

9

Gretchen Smith stared at the looming computer screens above her. Her hair had dried and she'd tied it up into a tight bun. She wore the only clothes she had on the station, a pair of blue jeans and a now lime green T-shirt.

She'd slipped on her tennis shoes and leather jacket as well. The cold metal station was a little too brisk for her comfort now.

The half-full bowl of chicken soup she'd had for, what she decided to call lunch, sat on the desk in front of her. It was difficult to tell time on a space station.

The bowl didn't let off any steam, it'd gone cold a while ago. It was far from the best soup she'd ever had. She was pretty sure the bits of chicken didn't originate from a living animal. The muscle fibers of the alleged meat were too evenly sized and dispersed, giving it a texture that was close but not quite accurate to real chicken.

Jupiter loomed in the window of the main atrium. She had watched it as she ate. The brown, red, yellow, and orange storm clouds moved slowly in front of her. It was like watching a fish tank at the doctor's office.

Then the computer had announced its completion of the USB port and sent her off across the station to pick it up from a manufacturing garage. What did this station not have?

It hadn't taken much to convince her to put down the pitiful soup. She also picked up her jacket and shoes while away from the desk. They were sitting in the spa, on the opposite side of the garage. Yet another trip across the station.

Traipsing back and forth reminded her of a two-story house Todd and she had lived in for a few years before deciding nothing would ever be on the right floor and vowing to only ever live in a single-story structure for the rest of their lives.

After following the computer's installation instructions she plugged in the USB. The computer scanned for viruses and analyzed the data. After a few minutes, it had pulled this up on screen.

And she didn't know what to do with it. Other than staring at it in bewilderment.

The screen was covered in text. She'd skimmed some of it. Concluded it was ridiculous.

Then she realized she was a time traveler on a space station, alone, at the end of time. Or at least near the end of the solar system.

The fact that the screen in front of her was detailed instructions for feeding, cleaning, and taking care of the purple heart machine that was recently delivered, shouldn't be that ridiculous. And that was just the first few pages of the documentation.

"How much of this is there?" Gretchen asked the station's AI computer.

"There are four manuals each about three hundred to four hundred pages of text."

Gretchen looked up and let out a groan that echoed through the empty metal room. Jupiter looked down at her, its giant storms indifferent to her frustration.

"Would you like me to summarize it for you?" The computer asked.

"Thank the gods. Yes, please!"

"All four manuals are written by Todd Rungson," the computer said. "It seems he built the contraption on an exoplanet of the Antares system a few hundred thousand years ago. Most of the information is related to caring for a younger state of the machine. We won't have to do much to maintain it now that it's here."

Todd had built something organic. On an exoplanet. He'd have to have an army of workers there helping him. Not completely unreasonable considering he was rich enough to have this space station.

"What's the machine used for?" Gretchen asked. The question had burned in her mind since she'd seen the hideous thing.

"It is made to manage human memories," the computer said.

"Can it remove them?" Gretchen asked. That was the reason she'd followed Todd after quitting her work with the avians. If the solution had landed in her lap she'd be free to travel the multiverse, free to go see this Pikowski person and maybe help Todd.

"Affirmative. It can delete, add, and update memories. It also seems to store them long term as well," the computer reported.

"Great! How do I use it?" Gretchen asked.

"The fourth manual in here is not a manual. It's a journal of Mr. Rungson's experience building the machine."

"Okay..."

"He seems to have lost his mind. Years worth of entries are nonsensical. It seems he was testing the machine on himself."

Gretchen sighed. "Did he get the bugs worked out? Is it safe to use?" she asked.

"Presently that's unclear. There are several diagnostics we can go through to make sure the machine is healthy. But based on what I'm reading in these files using the machine is risky."

Gretchen tapped her foot nervously under the desk. It was a solution to her problem. She could get the avian's tracking memory out of her mind. But she could go crazy in the process.

She wanted Todd here to at least ask him some questions.

"There are two memories stored in the machine already," the computer said, interrupting her thoughts. "It seems Todd wanted you to experience them before using the machine."

"Todd's memories?" Gretchen asked. "In my head? That's possible?"

Even if it was possible she wasn't sure she was comfortable with it. She'd lived hundreds of strange lives across time. But they'd all been her own.

"It is technically possible, based on Mr. Rungon's documentation. However, it hasn't been tested."

"Why not?" Gretchen asked.

"Mr. Rungson seems to have built this thing alone."

"Impossible!"

"I would be inclined to agree," the computer replied. "However in this universe, humanity was wiped out by the awakened beasts three billion years ago. Before this solar system's sun exploded. Mr. Rungson never mentions any other humans in his journal."

"He was alone on the planet? For how long? Developing something like this would take lifetimes," Gretchen said. Although of everyone in the multiverse Gretchen should've understood that Todd had lifetimes. Just didn't make it easy to wrap her head around the situation.

"Based on the descriptions of the night sky Todd leaves in the journals I can say it took him at least 500 years, give or take a few hundred since star dating is inclined to be inaccurate. Additionally, Todd's entries seem to be unreliable at times."

"So what are the memories he put in there?" She asked. Reluctant to be a guinea pig.

"That is not documented."

Gretchen wondered if they could be answers. Todd had never explained why he'd killed her across so many universes. Why she was given this ability to travel through the multiverse like him. She'd given up looking. She'd experienced enough loss in her lives to realize that knowing the answer wasn't necessary for healing.

Didn't make her less curious though. Given the opportunity.

But it could be risky. She could go crazy herself. Another person's memories in her mind. Would it be like watching a video or living their life?

She was immortal, for all intents and purposes, she was used to being able to stick forks in electrical sockets to find out what happens. But she'd never had to risk her sanity.

And who knew if Todd was coming back. Who knew if anyone would ever find this tiny satellite at the end of time. According to the computer, there were no humans in this universe. And the odds of a multidimensional traveler finding it on accident made looking for a needle in a haystack seem like a fun weekend project.

"Pull up Todd's journal," Gretchen finally told the computer. "I want to see what flavor of crazy we're working with."

She read.

She ordered a bowl of fried rice from the food generator.

She read some more.

The fried rice was better than the chicken noodle soup, if only because she opted for tofu.

The journal entries were not promising.

Most were detailed descriptions of the planet's flora and fauna. The human civilization there had left a diverse amount of life behind. According to Todd, it'd overtaken the buildings and city streets. Todd spent hours documenting the details of each plant he saw.

There were ravings of dreams he had. Dreams so realistic and accurate that she suspected they were dislodged memories. Especially because she hadn't had a dream since gaining her powers and the computer confirmed that Todd experienced the same. They spanned time. He bitched about historic monarchs, recounted space explorations, and recounted the intricacies and benefits of indoor plumbing at least three times.

The compassion Todd showed for the machine itself was remarkable to Gretchen. For the longest time, he was the man in her nightmares. But the way he spoke of and tended to the needs of the machine he was building was sweet.

He raised it like a pet or a child. It was some balance of the two. The machine was not sentient enough to be considered a peer but not as mindless and robotic as a computer. It could feel pain when he dismantled it for repair. It got sick and lethargic after a long day's work.

Seeing this side of Todd was strange to Gretchen. Through his words, she could separate him from the Todd she loved and grew old with. And his actions could separate him from the monster of her dreams. While she read the words on the screen she could see what the Gretchen who fell in love with him saw.

Gretchen read or had the computer read to her, for hours until she finally got drowsy enough that she wandered off to bed. The guest rooms of the satellite were similar to a hotel or cruise ship room. Comfortable enough despite their size, optimal for the space they had at their disposal.

She fell asleep peacefully. And had a dreamless sleep.

Which made the blaring alarms that woke her all the more jarring.

10

I stared at Pikowski's dead body. The singed hole in her chest smelled like burnt toast. The stunned expression on her face wanted me to give answers, closure. I could do neither now.

I had seen horrors before. I'd committed atrocities against people who didn't deserve it. Hell, I'd killed the man in front of me earlier today by slamming a coffee table on his chest.

But this hopeless shame I felt about Pikowski's death was the worst of it all. I'd dragged her into this investigation. I'd ignored her instructions not to touch the crystal. And I'd brought her to this gleaming pearlescent maze because of it.

I hadn't pulled the trigger. But I was responsible for putting her on the firing line.

"We don't need anyone else involved in our discussion," the killer said.

He was wearing a prim suit, tailored to fit his wiry body. His bowler hat sat perfectly level on his head. He looked like he was prepared to inspect some Victorian steel mill and listen to production reports. Have a mundane discussion about how many palettes were shipped out, what the quarterly profit and loss was, and how many street urchin fingers had gummed up the works in the past week.

He disgusted me. I'd kicked his ass once today. I considered doing it again.

"Come now," he commanded. "You two spent a good amount of time solving that maze. Not that we have a shortage of it. Let's have some tea and chat."

Of course, the bastard drank tea. Couldn't handle the intensity of coffee like a decent person.

He turned his back on me, the long tails of his suit jacket waggled as he walked away from the maze. His gait was uneven, just like in the security feed. The gun still in his hand swayed back and forth as he walked.

He was a head shorter than me. I could tackle him. Take him to the ground. Beat the snot out of him.

He might get a few good blows in. May even shoot a laser or two through me.

But worst of all, I'd get no answers. Answers Pikowski had now died for.

I followed. Resentfully.

The killer led me down a tapered hallway. It felt like I was walking inside of a conch shell. The heels of his polished shoes clacked on the hard pearlescent floor. My boot steps were a little deeper but just as loud. Other than that we traveled in silence.

The hallway tapered until I could reach the ceiling with a simple jump. At the end of the hallway was a circular door. It was ornamented with intricate spirals embossed on the pearlescent wall that surrounded it. The top center had a cinnamon bun-shaped pattern that seemed to spiral into itself forever. Down each curved side of the door loose meandering spirals swirled away from the center as if something was trying to claw its way out. The decoration was the same pearlescent as the wall, but the way the light hit it made it mesmerizing to look at.

The door itself was cinched shut like a bandit's purse. It was an opaque grey spiral of muscle that reminded me of a camera's aperture. As the killer approached the muscles loosened with an uncomfortable squelching sound. The killer passed under the door and I followed having to duck my head a bit to avoid hitting the top of the arch.

The room we walked into was a cacophony of animal noises and smells. I'd expected a house, a foyer, a wide-open field. Even a secretary's desk and waiting area would've been fine. Instead, I was greeted by beasts chirping, letting out deep bellows, or growling at me. The room smelled musty despite it being wide open to a domed ceiling that was at least nine stories high. It was certainly bigger than any environment dome I'd lived in while terraforming planets.

The beasts themselves were held back by a small pattern on the floor. One that I was familiar with because I'd just solved a maze built of the same domed markings and invisible walls that seemed to keep the things back.

Each beast was unrecognizable to me. One seemed to be a tiger with scales like a snake and the face of a mole. But even all those different combinations didn't do the alien thing justice. Another was as large as an elephant but instead of the baggy ears I'd come to expect it had tall ears like a rabbit. Its nose was long but resembled an arm more than the flimsy trunk I'd expect from a beast this size.

Then I saw a creature I recognized. Its holding area was next to a polished wooden coffee table with, as promised, a teapot and delicate tea cups. The creature sat behind an invisible wall, disinterested in the killer and me.

The humanoid shape split the difference between me and the killer. The stark black wings on its back would tower over me, even if they were folded up as tight as they could go. It had feathered arms with three dexterous yellow claws at the end of its hands. Its feet were clamped onto a bar that sat maybe a foot off the ground, and it squatted with a book resting on its knees. A purple sash crossed the bird-like humanoid's body, and I could tell some items were stored inside the sash's hidden pockets.

Its head was sleek like an eagle's. Its yellow beak and eyes were the only pop of color on its face. Its eyes were such a bright yellow that they looked like headlights made with phosphorescent lamps. The beak was smooth and came to a sharp point that made the talons look harmless. Humanity was the apex predator on Earth thanks to intelligence alone. Avians had our intelligence, at least, and multiple weapons built into their body. I didn't want to know how or why this predator was captured by my host.

Each animal was surrounded by an environment of its own, most of which were as alien and indescribable as the animals they held. But this avian had a familiar surrounding, or at least familiar enough that I could put it into words. Rows of bookshelves filled the small square it sat in. Colorful leather-bound books filled the shelves and stacks covered a few small tables. Other reading perches like the one the avian sat on were on the hardwood floor.

The avian's cage, taped off with the floor's domed pattern, wasn't much bigger than a walk-in closet. But the bookshelves didn't stop at the edges. Instead, they ran back in rows suddenly cut off when they reached the invisible wall. A table was held up with only two legs. The desktop, and books on top of it, went into the wall, then disappeared as if someone had sawed it in half. It stood straight and sturdy despite being held up by nothing.

The killer, more interested in his tea, stepped off the pearlescent floor and onto the ornate rug that sat under the wooden coffee table. He beckoned me to join him, and I complied if only out of curiosity regarding what he might have to say.

I noticed the rug was cut strangely along the edges, a domed mound seemed to cut off the Persian-inspired teardrop pattern in strange angles that no sane designer would've chosen. I stepped over the dome, half expecting to hit an invisible wall in the process.

My foot never hit a wall but as soon as it landed on the floor I found myself in a parlor rather than the pearlescent room filled with beasts. I couldn't see the avian or the scaled tiger. But the teapot and coffee table were still there. The rug's teardrop patterns were complete with tassels on the short ends.

Burgundy armchairs with padded wings near the head were on both sides of the coffee table. The backs rose up like a narrow heart. The killer took a seat in one and gestured to a matching chair across from him.

I sat on the edge of the armchair. Uninterested in getting too comfortable around the killer or his beasts. There were two doors in the room one behind me and one to my right. I doubted either would lead back to the room of creatures. The walls were adorned with paintings of scenic landscapes, none of which were familiar to me.

The killer set down his pistol and poured us dark amber tea that stood out on the fine white china he served it in. He took the cup and the saucer it sat on and leaned back on the chair. The steam coming from the cup wafted into his face, around his bulbous nose and his broom-like white mustache.

Still on the edge of my seat, leaning forward I looked at my drink then scowled back at him.

"You brought me here," I said. My voice sounded like a growl, uneven and unmeasured. "Killed my partner. Least you can do is give me some answers."

The killer took a loud sip of his tea and then set the saucer and cup down on the large armrest of the chair. "How much do you remember?" he asked.

"Let's act like I don't know anything," I said. Sounded like I'd be lucky. This villain might be in a monologuing mood.

"We're friends Todd," he said. "I wouldn't have known where to find you if we weren't. I wouldn't have killed you if we weren't."

"Were you friends with Pikowski?" I asked with a frustrated smirk.

He picked up his teacup with his left hand and held the saucer in place with his right. "No, suppose I'm not. Seemed like a lovely lady though. Quick with a gun. Very observant." He took a contemplative sip. "Well if we're *acting* like you don't know anything then I suppose I should introduce myself. I'm Dasco Penfield. We've known each other for an astonishingly long time."

I grunted in response. I'd never heard of the man or met him. At least not in the memories I had. Which according to Gretchen and the avian Woah-Te was not all of my memories. It was possible I was friends with this killer, for more reasons than one. And I didn't like the prospect of that.

"I gave you your powers Todd. Surely you remember that?" Dasco said.

I didn't. Up until recently, I hadn't know where they originated. The fiasco with Gretchen taught me that important lesson.

"It would be remarkable if I didn't remember that trauma," I said.

Dasco smiled a knowing smile, I'd never been good at poker and took a sip of tea. He set the cup down with a clink holding it in place with his right hand. "I knew you were going to take a little off the top. But it seems you clipped out too much." He sounded disappointed despite his wrinkled grin. "Young Todd, ever eager."

Do our powers just come from a chain of murderers and monsters? I wondered. Each person passed on trauma and harm to countless versions of someone across the multiverse until they woke up to the ability to travel through it. It sounded disgusting. I was ashamed to be a part of it after seeing the pain it'd caused Gretchen firsthand.

It must have shown because Dasco mirrored my discomfort, if only superficially.

"How'd you do it?" I asked.

"You wouldn't believe me if I told you," Dasco replied. "You'll figure it out in due time. I've brought you here for other business."

It was clear conducting business with this man would wind up with one of us short-changed. As much as I wanted to screw him over, I doubted I'd get out of this transaction scot-free.

"Let's hear it," I said.

"Well as you saw walking through my zoo I'm a bit of a collector of beasts. All these beasts naturally interact with or control their conscious body. You do remember that part, right?"

I did but only because Gretchen had told me about it before returning my powers that she'd stolen with a worm she called a nitthog. She said living things have a physical body and a conscious body usually so tightly knit together that when one dies the other dies as well. But me, Dasco, Gretchen, and allegedly the other beasts in the zoo had the ability to hold our conscious body together after death.

I nodded and Dasco continued. "I need your help adding a beast to my collection."

I laughed out loud at the ridiculousness of the request. At what had led up to this request. "You killed me, twice, killed my friend, transported me to–" I gestured at the room, unsure of the word for where we were. "All so we could what? Go interdimensional-lion hunting?"

Dasco grinned, apparently able to see the humor where I only saw ridiculousness. He took a final sip of his tea. Set the empty cup on the table. Reached into his jacket pocket and pulled the crystal necklace out by the cord.

"Just consider the offer. This beast makes lions look like house cats. It might be fun and... I'd owe you one," he said with a mischievous grin.

Before I could say anything else he slung the necklace at me. The crystal came hurtling at me like a torpedo. I put my hands up to stop it from pelting me between the eyes.

As soon as I grabbed it grey static made the edges of my vision go fuzzy. I had more questions for my "old friend" Dasco. But he was already standing up from his chair. Before he stepped off the rug he'd left the room, through no door I could see.

My vision was overwhelmed by the grey static and the armchair was no longer under me. My stomach was in my throat. It felt like I was falling through nothing. And this time I had more questions than answers.

11

Monika's heart burned like the fire of a thousand suns. She clutched for her chest and, where she expected a bullet wound, she found the pocket of her faux leather vest.

With thin blue gloves back on her hands she frisked her body to make sure all her limbs and organs were accounted for and in the proper location.

She was alive.

She stood in the bloody living room of Todd Rungson. Her heart raced and she fought to catch her breath. But a racing heart was better than a bleeding heart. Her nerves were on edge and every sound made her jump.

So when, out of nowhere, Mr. Rungson appeared centimeters away from her she had his hand wrenched behind his back before either of them knew what was going on.

She let go and he fell to the ground. He was in a long leather coat, thick boots, and heavy blue pants. He looked up at her, the unfamiliar scruff on his cheeks and shocked brown eyes were the opposite of any photo she'd seen of the Conglomerate Head.

She offered him a hand up. He took it and rubbed his wrist where she had grabbed him.

"Are you okay?" She asked.

"Are you?" he asked with a hesitant smile. "Last I saw you there was a hole the size of my fist in your chest."

"Blessed Elders, that happened then?" The last thing she remembered was pulling her gun on the killer who had revealed a firearm from behind his back. There was a flash of light and heat, and then she was here. "Why am I not dead?" she asked.

Her gun was still in its holster, the gloves she'd taken off when she appeared in the maze were on her hands. But it was as if she'd never left this room.

She let out a yawn, there was a crime scene that still needed to be wrapped up and then cleaned up. It'd be the start of her next shift before she got to her apartment. Kot wouldn't be happy she'd worked this late.

"Your guess is as good as mine," Rungson said, unhelpfully. "Cosmic consciousness and all that. If you start having dreams of suicide or no dreams at all let me know."

"Why?" Monika rarely remembered her dreams. And suicidal thoughts had left once she quit her previous job a dozen years ago.

"No reason," Rungson said. He wasn't trying to hide that he was hiding something. "But I met my killer, apparently we're old pals this was his way of saying hello I guess. I'll have a team clean up the bodies if you're done with the scene."

"I've got a few more things to check. I'd like to have an autopsy of..." She looked at the bodies. A second autopsy of the Conglomerate Head in just as many days would be suspicious. And if the killer wasn't registered in any of Griffith's databases that'd add even more questions.

"You want an autopsy?" Rungson said, not unkindly. "Cause of death is clear. You'll find I had a blood alcohol level a hair past sober, and no other narcotics in my system. Doubt the killer had any time to get stoned in the short time he was here–"

"It's fine," Monika said. "The necklace though. I'd like to catalog it with the other evidence I've collected."

Rungson handed her an empty plastic bag. On the outside, in her loopy handwriting, the case number, date, and contents of the bag were filled out. Other than that it was empty. Rungson halfheartedly patted down his pockets. "I don't have it either."

She shook her head in disappointment. There were procedures. But Rungson was too important to follow them. She'd pull herself from the case if it wasn't so high profile. She'd chew him out if...

"Wait, so we're done here?" she asked. "You found your killer. He's a friend. How the hell am I going to explain this to the media, to Chief Stone, to forensics?"

"I appreciate your help," Rungson said. "I'll have a PR team come up with a spin for the story. A privatized cleaning crew can get my living room cleaned up by morning. I'll tell Stone you did great work, hell you died mid-investigation. They still give out medals for that kind of stuff?"

Rungson was grinning now, having a good time, ignorant of the fact that it'd been painful to get shot. She saw dead bodies every day, saw the life drained from friends and innocent people over meaning-less squabbles. And this man treated it like it was a joke.

"Do you realize the chaos you've brought into this world? You died, we had half the force over here. People who could've been on the streets keeping other people safe. People who needed it. People who aren't just going regenerate after death."

She stepped away from him. Walked between the bodies to the other side of the living room just to get away from him.

"You have more power than the Elders, than God, than every conglomerate in the system combined. Yet you treat it like it's some kind of joke? You use this world, hell probably all the worlds under Rungson, as your personal playground. Despite what CS wants people to believe there are still people starving, dying, and getting addicted to drugs out on the streets. And you what showed up here to catch up with an old pal? It's disgusting."

Monika let out an exasperated sigh. Looked away from Rungson who wasn't nearly shocked enough. Her eyes rested on a statue that was so ugly that only someone with more money than sense would like it.

She wanted to knock it over, rebel, piss Rungson off to get a response. But tipping the statue over would ruin the preservation of the crime scene.

"You're right," Rungson said. "I could spend a dozen lifetimes on improving Griffith and then another dozen on every other planet under the Rungson Conglomerate. I should. I have a friend that'd be glad you were chewing me out. For what that's worth."

"Then why don't you?" Monika said. The question came out sharp but his admission of guilt had taken the teeth out of her accusation. "Bigger fish to fry?" She used the antiquated phrase mockingly. But even that sounded hollow.

"I have a hard time seeing the little guys. Can you imagine every bug on this planet? Could you imagine making sure every one of them was happy and healthy? I'm sorry for the comparison, but that's what it feels like to me."

Monika looked to the Conglomerate Head. His gaze was focused on the blank TV, thoughtful and regretful. She'd seen it before, on a case where a boy had gotten into his parent's cleaning supplies and accidentally poisoned himself because of it.

"I'm trying to do better," he said.

A lot of people had lied to her about a lot of things over the years. Right now Rungson wasn't one of them.

"Good," she said. It was sharp but she tried to pad it. "The bugs appreciate it."

Rungson's stupid grin was back on his face. She'd never desired to be as powerful as a Conglomerate Head. She hardly envied Chief Stone for his power and authority. But to see the weight of power resting on Rungson's shoulders she was grateful for her mortality. Dying twice would be plenty for her.

"Anything I can do specifically for you?" Rungson asked. "I can book you a trip to Feldman's like we talked about. I can make up a medal or new position in the police force for you."

Monika peeled her blue gloves off and dropped them next to Rungson's dead body. It landed on a pile of bags she'd put together earlier. Bags that'd be taken care of by some privatized clean-up crew.

She shook her head as she passed him. "Just keep the drama to a minimum."

"I'll do my best," Rungson said.

Monika navigated her way out of the big house while Rungson made a call to the clean-up crew. She was looking forward to getting back home. Getting to Kot and her comfortable bed. If she was lucky she wouldn't have to deal with Rungson for the rest of her life.

12

I had no shortage of work to do. Monika, her fiery temper a harsh but welcome wake-up call, had some good points. The death of a leader might be a good opportunity to make some reforms. Plus, I still had to put together a design for the USB drive. Which would be an exhausting amount of traveling back and forth from my timeline to this one.

That was a task that would be significantly easier with a perfect memory.

I got to work once the clean-up crew arrived. They'd dispose of the bodies. They were paid well enough to ask no questions. I wondered what other kinds of people used this service. Wondered how different I was from others who needed bodies gone without question.

I doubted all their customers were time travelers with undocumented bodies that needed to disappear before more questions could be raised.

These thoughts and musings came to me as I had a shave. The auto-groomer did most of the work. It did my hair as well, wrestling the tangled mess into a neatly combed and gelled mass. My cheeks only had a few nicks once it was all over. I wasn't used to sitting still while blades flurried around me.

Finished in the bathroom, I put on the dark blue and slightly less chaotically patterned button-up shirt and a long robe-like cloak and headed to the office for the real work. A large black marble desk with a terminal computer embedded into the desk's top sat in the center of the room. Two bookshelves, also made of black marble, held rare paper books. It was on my right when sitting at the desk. In front of the desk, two hand-carved wooden chairs with black cushions faced me, their back to the door. They were the largest wood pieces on the property, maybe in the whole capital city. To my left, a short black credenza with a glass cabinet mounted on top held a number of other remarkable valuables, including an empty stand that once held a sharp hunting knife.

Dasco wanted me to go on a hunt with him. However, he didn't strike me as a man who made offers without strings attached. He showed up and killed me, as a friend. Who knew what he'd do with his enemies. And I didn't remember enough about our relationship to know how close I was to that line.

I took a deep breath. One thing at a time. Figure out what was on the USB drive. Get back to the Fortress with Gretchen. I could decide to hunt with Dasco another time. It's not like either of us were going to run out of it.

I traveled back and forth in time. In my original timeline, or at least close enough, I learned about USB drive manufacturing and protocols for reading it. I memorized the information as best I could. Then I traveled back to my office on Griffith and transposed the information into the desk's terminal.

The cleaning crew came and went. Night turned into early morning then early morning turned into afternoon. And all of that time felt like a month to me as I spent large periods of time in the past studying Universal Serial Bus, and the storage devices attached to them.

My body didn't feel particularly tired, but my mind was exhausted. I packaged it up in a text file as that would be easiest to encode and transmit. Between that and the wardrobe work order for Gretchen my work in this universe was done. At least the work I'd originally set out to do.

But Pikowski was right. As the head of the Rungson conglomerate, I could do better. I began looking into what it would take to reform the city, planet, and conglomerate as a whole. I went through old theories I'd learned in high school were failed experiments. I looked into new research and approaches. Learned about the kritarchy of the Central System, the benefits of Minister judges, and their downsides. It didn't take me long to realize that even as an immortal this would be a time-consuming task.

A knock on the door interrupted my research. It was evening. My stomach growled for food. My head ached from a long day of work. My body longed to move out of the chair and office it'd been confined to all day. I looked up. Whoever had knocked didn't wait to be let in.

Dasco, in his bowler hat, fine suit, and polished shoes that made a click-clack on the white tile floor of the office entered. He still favored his left foot as he walked. But this time he had a thin black cane. The pommel of the cane was a silver cobra ready to strike. The only thing more intimidating than the snake was the bulbous laser gun he pointed at me. The smile he wore didn't do enough to make him feel innocuous.

I took a deep breath. With all the traveling I'd done today I already had a foot out the door.

The terminal in front of me rang.

"I'll let you take that," Dasco said, still pointing the pistol at me. He approached my desk, took a seat in one of the wooden chairs in front of me. He leaned his cane between his leg and armrest, took his bowler hat off, and set it on my desk. The skin of his bald head glared white with the office's overhead lights.

Chief Stone was calling. Likely about Pikowski's work. I hadn't gotten back to him since closing the case. I was waiting for her to finish her part of the paperwork. I'd rubber stamp it with accolades for her. She'd have a remarkable career ahead of her with my endorsement.

I could escape. Call Stone back later. Dasco encouraged me to pick up with the tip of his gun.

I answered the call. Stone appeared on my screen, clean-shaven but worn down everywhere else. His black hair with streaks of grey was a mess. His colorful shirt was unbuttoned the top few buttons and he hadn't put on an overcoat.

I didn't look significantly better, but I was in charge. The luxuries of leadership.

Pikowski stood behind the chief her short black bangs were just barely out of frame. Despite being up late last night and already working late today she looked as orthogonal as ever. She wore a newly styled garment, a combination of overalls and a skirt with a frilly blouse underneath it. Fashion looks strange when you're out of your time period. I have trouble getting used to it, but Pikowski looked nice nonetheless.

"Need something from me to wrap up my murder?" I asked. "My father's murder," I corrected.

"No," Stone said. "That's been put on the back rack. We've got a series of attacks that Pikowski thinks you can help on. I apologize for reaching out to you. Normally we would take care of this kind of thing without getting you involved. I'm sure you're busy with your father's affairs, funeral, and grieving…"

Stone continued on for a while as I wondered if that was something I should do for myself. At the very least I should get some department of the conglomerate to take care of it. I'd hate to look too much like a heartless bastard. Especially since I was trying to have this generation of Conglomerate Head appear more philanthropic and interested in the plight of the people.

"There have been a series of animal attacks," Chief Stone continued. "Animals inside the city are strange enough. Based on the security footage they're not a native species either."

I nodded, still not seeing why I was being dragged into this.

"Their appearance on the security footage is abnormal. Forensics is having a tough time with it. Well, I'll just show you." Chief Stone sent a video file to me and it automatically played on my terminal screen.

A woman walked down the sidewalk towards the security camera. Based on my angle it was likely mounted on a lamppost. She carried a shopping bag and wore an overall skirt like Pikowski, with a low-cut T-shirt underneath. She sang along to some music only she could hear. She was a fairly good singer, but only the security camera was there to appreciate it. Her hair was long and curly and a bit frizzed, but not unkempt, from the day she'd had.

Out of nowhere a misshapen monkey with leathery skin like a lizard appeared on the sidewalk. It lumbered up to her on all fours like a gorilla. She screamed, dropped her bag, and started to run.

The camera feed switched to a different perspective. From the new angle, I could clearly watch the lizard-like monkey jump on her back and tackle her to the ground. It took a bite out of her shoulder and clung onto her scalp and arm with its hands as if it were trying to keep her still.

Without any more effort on the monkey's part, the woman went limp on the sidewalk. There was no pool of blood, no ripping of guts, it was as if she'd passed out. Strangely, the monkey wasn't acting like a beast looking for food.

The monkey lifted its head out of her neck and took a few steps on its hind legs like it was strolling to the corner store for a sandwich. It seemed to be humming or chirping a tune. With one of its steps, it blipped out of existence the same as it had appeared.

"The creature does the same thing your killer did," Pikowski said leaning down to look into the chief's camera. Her black bangs and short hair framed her stern gaze. "Anything you know?"

"I don't know much," I said. "But I've got a friend here who might." I gave her a hesitant grin.

Pikowski returned my smile with a bit of shock and concern. "You having a party? Should we join you?"

Chief Stone seemed to be offended on my behalf for how friendly the detective was being.

"No, no," I said with a polite chuckle. "Just us two should be enough fun for me. I'll call you back with what I know."

I looked up to Dasco. He was holstering the gun under his suit jacket. He smiled at me.

"Sounds like I'm going hunting with you after all," I said.

13

Dasco looked across the desk at me. His ice-blue eyes felt like they were a trap. A glacier ready to sink a boat. A mountainside ready to become an avalanche.

I didn't know what to think about the lizard monkey that I'd just watched attack an innocent woman on the streets of Griffith's capital city. Chief Stone hadn't know what to do with it either. Pikowski was the only one who could connect anything, and even that was just her bringing the problem to me.

Should I regret having told her about my abilities? I wouldn't be roped into this if I had kept the information to myself. I wouldn't have to worry about innocent civilian deaths.

But that wasn't the person I wanted to be. That's not the version of me that Gretchen wants me to be. The one able to travel the multiverse. Not the one whom I spent a lifetime with. Although she probably believed I was a decent person, maybe she'd want me to be this way too.

Getting myself wrapped up with Dasco, the sharply dressed alleged friend of mine, seemed like a bad idea. My memories were gone, unable to be stored long term, or at least as long term as my immortal life needed them to be stored.

Had he done that to me? Perhaps he wiped all the memories that would convince me not to partner up with him and go hunting these deadly monkeys. And I was helpless to remember the facts. All my brain could do was send shivers down my spine every time I looked at him.

"Can you help me hunt down these monkeys?" I asked.

"No," Dasco said. The word was flat like a professor delivering a rote fact.

"You're obviously well versed in these kinds of creatures–"

"I want your help hunting a beast that eats these monkeys for breakfast," Dasco said interrupting me.

The little devil took down the woman in seconds. Seemed to render her lifeless without much more than a bite and a scratch. I could only imagine how what the beast that ate them for breakfast might be like.

"The monkeys are called lefths," Dasco said. "They have the ability to control their conscious body and travel through the multiverse like us. They usually aren't particularly intelligent. There are not many of them so they don't appear in a lot of timelines. However, once one finds a meal in a timeline it leaves a trail back to other lefths. Leading to swarms of them."

"Which explains the multiple attacks Stone was talking about," I said.

"And this is just the beginning." Dasco was grinning his devilish grin despite the weight of the situation. "There will be a swarm of them here within the week if not sooner."

I pushed my hair back. It was still slick with musky gel but its hold was starting to fade. The long day of work had done a number on it. This lefth situation wasn't going to make it better.

I could abandon Griffith. It'd be a shame since this is the universe my Fortress of Solitude is in hovering around Jupiter after humanity's extinction. But I could make another. There were infinite universes for me to make a home in.

But I'd just told Pikowski I was trying to do better. And my experience with Gretchen, seeing the many lives I'd lived despite knowing I was the one living them, still haunted me. I couldn't abandon these bugs to an anteater. Not without a fight.

"There's no way to protect a whole timeline from them?" Dasco continued. "But we can bring in something bigger to clean them up and keep them out. And it just so happens my collection is wanting for the beast who can do this."

"What's that one called? A Righth?" I asked, never too busy to make a joke.

Dasco gave me a faint smile of appreciation but nothing more. "It's called a Garmound and it'd be easier if I showed you." He stood up, leaning on the desk instead of his cane. He reached inside his jacket and I half expected him to shoot me for the "fun" of it. Instead, he placed a necklace on the desk.

This one was held by the same natural cordage as the crystal necklace. Except instead of a crystal on the end it had a wooden coin. A symbol I didn't recognize was carved into the face of the coin. It looked most like the traces of a circuit board. The cord looped through a hole at the top of the coin.

I reached for the coin interested in inspecting it closer. Dasco put his slender fingers around it like a cage, but he didn't touch the coin.

"Touch me," he said, "I'll touch the coin."

I did as much, wrapping my hand around his wrist. He pressed his palm flat on the desk and the edges of my vision became fuzzy with static. Soon enough my desk chair felt like it had slipped out from under me. I was falling ass first through the multiverse.

And then my butt hit the ground, cushioned by the grass of a green meadow. There was a beautiful purple sky above me. It was midday and the red giant star loomed above us in the sky.

Dasco still wore his suit, bowler hat, and his cobra cane was back under his hand. But now a crystal necklace hung around his neck.

I wore my traveling clothes, my long jacket heavy on my shoulders and warm for the seemingly summer day.

We were on top of a hill covered in green grass. Hills surrounded us with small square dots on them. They seemed like buildings, or at least were buildings at one point in time. Now they only housed vegetation like climbing vines and sprawling shrubs. The grass wasn't a variation I was familiar with, it curled like locks of hair giving it an almost moss-like texture, and it grew thick enough that I couldn't see the dirt underneath. I stood up and smelled something floral in the air. My stomach groaned and I wish I'd had something quick to eat, I'd settle for something as simple as a roast beef sandwich.

I took a deep breath. I could feel my location in the multiverse and could find my way back to my office on Griffith. This time the necklace hadn't taken away my ability to travel.

"Where are we?" I asked. "Why use a necklace to travel?" I wondered if these were the kinds of questions I once knew the answer to but had forgotten. Things Dasco had taught me as a mentor or friend.

"An exoplanet in the Antares system, the garmound's home. Or at least one of them," Dasco said. "Necklaces make it hard for things to follow you. You really have forgotten quite a lot."

"When you get to be my age your memory just isn't what it used to be," I said. This did get an amused smile out of Dasco, but not much more. "Is being followed something likely to happen?" I asked. I knew that Gretchen talked about the avians implanting a tracking memory in her mind. And now lefths could leave trails for others of their kind.

Maybe like tracking game, the trail was obvious once you knew where to look.

Dasco shrugged as an answer. "Better safe than sorry. There are nasty things out there. The garmound being one of them."

I noticed a trail in the green grass. It was made of flat stones that seemed to be embedded in the grass, like a tree growing around a bolt placed into the trunk. My eyes followed it to a building at the bottom of the hill. I began walking that way following the path.

"Stay close," Dasco said. He was walking towards me his cane sinking into the grass doing little to help him. He seemed to be favoring it more than he did before our fight. I wondered if my kick at his leg had done more to hurt him than the coffee table. "If the garmound appears your breath won't get you out of here fast enough."

"Then what will?" I asked as Dasco approached me on the flat stones.

He dangled his crystal necklace by the cord once his polished black shoes were on the stone path. His cane leaned firm on the stone. "You better be touching me before I touch this."

"Might as well lock hands like Dorthy and the Scarecr–"

The call of a bugle interrupted me and I turned to look at it. On the side of the hill next to us a bipedal bird that looked like the giant version of a roadrunner darted across the green hill. The only reason I didn't think it was a road runner, aside from the size, was that instead of a narrow bird-like beak it had a long shield-like nose that rose past its forehead and behind its head like an inverted horn. But like a roadrunner, it had a massive plume of bright orange tail feathers that it used to help it steer as it darted across the hillside. The rest of their feathers were darker browns and amber.

A half dozen more followed it appearing out of nowhere. Each one letting out a screeching bugle call. It sounded like a dozen kindergartners were given whistles and all they could do was blow a single out-of-tune note.

A half dozen became a dozen and two dozen all appearing as if they'd walked through an invisible doorway. It was hard to tell each individual bird apart from this distance and with how tightly they ran together as a pack.

The bugle calls were overshadowed, but not stopped, by a new sound. A deep roar echoed through the hills. Bounding from higher on the hill appeared a jet-black quadrupedal beast bounding down the hill toward the birds.

The flock turned to run down the hill to avoid the beast who would flank them if they didn't.

Dasco grabbed my wrist. His cane clinked to the ground. I looked at him and he watched the new creature chase the birds. His hand hovered over his chest ready to clutch his necklace like an old woman hearing a rumor about her granddaughter. "That's the garmound," he said.

I looked back to the beast. Its four thick legs had wide paws like a lion. Its face was sharp like a wolf's. That was where the similarities ended. It had tail-like tentacles coming out of its shoulders and hips. They whipped around in the air as it chased the beasts.

One tentacle hit a lagging bird. Amber feathers puffed into the air. The bird went down and the beast pounced on it. The bugle sounds began to fade the flock was disappearing as if walking through another invisible doorway.

The garmound unhinged its jaw and bit into the bird like it was an apple. It took a few bites then stopped to look around as if it was worried something would steal its lunch. Dasco tightened his grip on my wrist.

The garmound disappeared without a step.

A roar proceeded its appearance in front of me. Its sharp wolf-like face looked down on me with dark mossy green eyes. Up close the beast seemed as big as a house. It had strong shoulders with rippling muscle and short fur that stood on edge around the flurry of tentacles. The garmound's unhinged jaw showed a light pink pallet of gums that held needle-like teeth around the edges. Teeth also ran down the center of its top and bottom jaws. Which was confusing, until it split its jaw vertically and its mouth opened like a flower. Two thin snake-like tongues shot out at me. I wasn't sure if they were going to slice at me or strangle me.

It didn't matter. My view of the beast and the green hills around it was covered with gray static. I fell as if the floor dropped out from under me, and the terrifying sensation of falling through the multiverse was a relief.

14

We stood in the pearlescent maze. My heart raced in my chest. Dasco let go of my wrist. The salty fishy stench of the room, almost unnoticeable the first time I'd been transported here, was a stark contrast to the floral smell of the hilly planet. The silence of the room, only interrupted by Dasco's cane tapping the ground with every step, was a relief to the garmound's roar that I could still hear in my ears.

The room was shimmering with purple, cream, and pink. Dasco had begun working his way through the maze, quicker than Pikowski and I's slow attempt. I jogged a bit to catch up but he hadn't made it far.

Dasco solved the maze without hitting any dead ends. If I had a perfect memory like Gretchen claimed she did then I would know how to get in if I ever found myself here. Unfortunately, the left and right turns did not stick in my memory. But it was an interesting security measure.

"You want to let that thing loose in the city?" I asked. "How would you even go about catching one of those things?"

Dasco silently stepped through the aperture door, I ducked to avoid hitting my head on the ornamented frame.

"How do you catch any of these things?" I asked as we walked into the zoo. Strange creatures stood all around me. They were once disgusting and terrifying. Compared to the garmound I'd just faced now they were just disgusting. And that was merely because they went against my expectations. With time I might consider them normal.

Dasco silently made his way toward his parlor. The crooked carpet and coffee table sat inside a raised ledge. He didn't step into it. Instead, he walked past it and into the cage of the black avian bird I'd noticed earlier. I followed and the shimmering pearlescent room disappeared.

I stood in the middle of a massive cylindrical room that smelled musty like leather and old paper. The domed roof above let blue light in through the tinted glass and it made the room feel like it was under-water. A mezzanine wrapped around the ground floor that Dasco, the bird, and I stood on. Both levels had wooden bookshelves filled with colorfully bound books, more than anyone could read in a lifetime. Maybe more than I could read in my long life.

Four hallways ran orthogonal to each other away from the center of the circular observatory, filled with even more books. The ground floor had a few tables for study, each one covered in books. Little bars, about a foot off the ground, were around the tables. The avian was perched on one a book balancing on their knees.

"Tooodd good to see you again," the jet-black avian said to me. The way the avian pronounced my name had a bit of a whistle to it inside the drawn-out syllable.

"Our friend's memory is... lacking in certain places," Dasco explained to the avian. "This is Swee Pip," Dasco made a popping sound with his lips as he pronounced the word. "She helps me with research into multidimensional beasts and situations."

The bird's beak and talons were bright yellow, a purple sash was slung across her chest and hung unevenly, weighed down by something in the pockets. She set the book she was reading down and stepped off her perch. Her looming black wings shifted back and forth to help her balance as she stood up. She reached out a taloned hand to shake mine. I took it, hesitantly.

Swee Pip whistled as she pondered Dasco's statement. The sounds were distinctly bird-like, as expected, and nothing I could produce with my lips. "Are we looking to remedy that?" she asked.

"Not at this moment," Dasco said. "Right now he's got a lefth infestation building in a universe he *cares* about," Dasco said with sharp almost insulting disdain for the concept. As if I was helping an injured puppy find a vet and that wasn't a noble action in his eyes.

Swee Pip whistled some more, this time it was higher pitched and Dasco replied with a slight smile. Maybe it was a laugh, the avian's beak had no flexibility to communicate a smile.

"I wouldn't mind clearing up the memory situation," I said. "It's a real shame I can't remember any of the good times we all had... as friends." I smiled with this and Swee Pip repeated her higher-pitched whistle.

"Good times indeed," the avian said punctuating the statement with a quick clicking sound. With a quick flap of her looming black wings, she hopped from the ground floor to the second floor perching on the banister and pacing back and forth on it as she leaned over to examine the book on the shelves.

"Do we really have time to dig into your memory problem?" Dasco asked, his voice low almost a growl as if he didn't want the avian to hear from the second floor.

Swee Pip whistled an upbeat tune as she searched the records. Either ignorant of our conversation or uninterested.

"You and I don't really have a shortage of time," I retorted my voice low and matching his but without the growl.

"You wiped your own memory. If you forgot why then there's probably a reason." Dasco replied. "You didn't give me much information about why you were doing it either."

I'd wiped my own memory. Dasco had made a comment like that on our first meeting. I hadn't thought much of it. I left no memories about forgetting though. And I'd gone to town wiping them out. Plus I'd placed a block to make old memories fade.

Of course, if Dasco wiped my memory he could say anything he wanted to. I had no evidence to hold against him. And despite killing me he didn't want me dead. He could've left me in front of the garmound back there. Instead, he brought me to Swee Pip who could hopefully help with the lefths and the memories. I was beginning to trust Dasco. And as comfortable as it was to have a friend, it still felt like I was sleeping in a wolf's den.

Swee Pip hopped off the banister of the second floor and glided down to our level catching herself on one of the perches. She stepped off and handed me a stack of books. "These are the books I gave you when you came to me asking about memories of the consciousness the first time. Should've known you were up to something." She punctuated the statement with a high-pitched whistle, maybe another laugh, or an inflection of disappointment, or a clue she was using sarcasm. There was no way for me to tell.

"Now on to the lefth situation," she marched off to a shelf on the ground floor.

"We'd like to use a garmound to clear them out," Dasco added as I flipped through the book.

Most of it was written in sharp scratches where every letter looked like a u, n, c, or a backward c. There were a few images of organs and veins which didn't look like human anatomy, maybe it described one of the creatures in Dasco's zoo.

"I can't read this Swee Pip." I tried to make the popping sound with my lips like Dasco did but it felt awkward.

"Oh you really ruffled up all your feathers," Swee Pip said handing Dasco a few books. "Makes sense if Dasco here has finally convinced you to catch him a garmound."

I looked to Dasco to see how he handled the accusation. He was unaffected and placed the books Swee Pip had given him on an open spot at the same table as me. He took a deep breath as if to explain.

A chair appeared behind him.

It was identical to the chairs in my office from the black cushion to the details of the ornately carved legs.

"Did you just steal my chair?" I asked frustrated by Dasco's aloofness. "I'm sick of being left in the dark. I want answers. How do I know you two didn't wipe my memories yourself? This could all just be a ruse to get me to help you capture another prized animal for your zoo."

Swee Pip's wings folded into her back and she looked smaller than me for once. Dasco on the other hand only reacted with his stupid devilish smile then opened his book turning his attention to it.

I took a step towards him and shut the book with a slam. "I'm serious. I want answers!"

Dasco looked up. If I'd frustrated him he didn't show it. His face was serious as if delivering a lesson to a child.

"If I had the ability to wipe your memory I'd do it to myself," he said. "And quite frankly, I'm a little miffed that you are unwilling to share the technology."

15

The satellite's alarms blared, jarring Gretchen awake. At first, she thought it was a smoke alarm. They used to go off randomly when she lived with Todd in that cheaply built two-story house they started out in. But the polished silver walls of the small room and the empty spot next to her in bed put that theory to rest quite quickly. She was clearly in a hotel. No, a bedroom on Todd's, the time-traveling one, satellite home.

And something had hit the fan.

There was no explanation of the alarm just a constant blaring. She could hardly hear herself think. The TV that sat across from the bed flashed red and white fast enough to get her attention, maybe even fast enough to give someone a seizure.

In black text, it read: EVACUATE IMMEDIATELY

Evacuate to where? Jupiter? She could disappear with a breath but that'd put an army of avians on her trail in no time. They'd bring her back to the Mother Tree. They may even try to serve her some justice, and she certainly didn't want to be on the wrong end of their talons.

Gretchen slid out of bed pulled on her pants and slipped into her shoes. Her leather jacket was hung over the back of an armchair and she shrugged it on over her now red shirt. Red. That made sense considering the circumstances.

Her grandmother's watch, with its shattered face, dangled around her left wrist. She was comfortable enough with that to sleep with it on. The purple tattoo on the other wrist wouldn't come off without some coaxing.

Something smelled awful she couldn't quite put her finger on the source. Maybe it was coming from the en suite bathroom.

"Computer what's going on?" she shouted over the blaring alarm making her way out of the bedroom and into the cramped living room of her current living quarters. The kitchenette still had leftovers from her dinner. Maybe that's what was giving off the rotten stench. Funny how something could be freeze-dried for centuries and then go bad overnight.

The TV that was mounted across from the couch was flashing red and white with the same unhelpful words. The computer responded. Its monotone voice gave her bits of information between blares of alarms. But she couldn't understand any of it.

"Turn the damn alarms off," she commanded. Half the time she left the smoke alarms stacked in the laundry room or wrapped in grocery bags to keep them from going off.

The room went quiet. Gretchen took a deep breath to relax. The urge to travel was there. She could escape this strange station. But the risk was too great.

"What were you saying?" she asked the computer.

"There's an anomaly with the oxygen levels on the station. I'm required to inform you to evacuate immediately. There are escape shuttles at the exterior ring of the station."

"Evacuate until you can fix it?" she asked starting a jog down the hallway towards the outer ring.

"Negative. All my systems report they are functioning fine. There is nothing I can do to rectify the problem."

"Then what? I float around Jupiter until I starve?" Gretchen was out of breath as she got to the bright yellow door labeled: Escape Shuttles.

"You got space suits in this place?" she asked while panting and pulling her hair back into a ponytail. It was so strange to be this out of breath, it felt like she'd run a marathon, not a few yards down a hall. She wasn't out of shape, not in a version of her body that was this young.

"They're near the evacuation shuttles." A cabinet door popped open next to the yellow door. "However, there are none in your size. I would recommend you do not over-exert yourself and immediately enter the pod. The oxygen levels are dropping rapidly."

"You know what they say about lemons and lemonade," she said. She regretted taking such deep breaths. Her nose and mouth filled with the stench of sewage. It smelled like a black water pipe had busted.

Looking into the closet a half dozen identical garments hung inside. They looked more like wet suits than the thick space suits she'd grown up seeing astronauts use. But a row of helmets, slightly thinner than motorcycle helmets, seemed to indicate that there were still some similarities.

She slipped out of her jacket and shoes and pulled the baggy suit on over her shirt and jeans. The computer urged her to get into the escape pod the entire time. She ignored it. She couldn't do anything floating around in space.

The elastic fabric of the suit crinkled with every movement. The fabric hung low under her arms and the waist hit her at her upper thighs. She felt like a baby inside a toddler's onesie. She was confounded by Todd's hubris to put one size of space suit on the ship. That'd be like filling a cruise ship with only extra large life jackets. It showed a real commitment to solitude. Which reminded Gretchen that there were some similarities between him and her Todd.

She twisted the helmet on and it locked in place connecting with the metal ring around her neck. The ring hung low like a necklace and she had to hold the helmet in place to keep it from tipping backwards or forwards. There was a hissing sound in her ear. The sound stopped. Then restarted. The pattern repeated a few times, frustratingly. She could breathe a little easier but the sewage smell was still there.

"Please put on the boots to complete the seal," the computer said in her ear. The glass face mask showed a bright yellow circle around the bottom of the closet where she'd grabbed the helmet. Behind the empty slot of her helmet were two boots. Both had similar metal rings that could connect to the suit's leg cuffs.

At least Todd had bigger feet than her. He'd be screwed if the sizes were reversed. She slipped the boots on and locked them in place at the ankles, not easy to do with the suit's gloves. The gloves were slightly more maneuverable than thick ski gloves but not by much. There was a hiss next to her ear and this time it cut off with a slurp of suction. The sewage smell disappeared and was replaced with cool sterile air like she was standing in front of an AC vent at a hospital.

An indicator at the bottom of her glass face shield was green and showed 96% O2. The air supply must be coming from the small backpack that was embedded into the suit. It was no bigger than a grocery bag and it hung awkwardly on her back. If the suit was the right size she suspected it'd sit comfortably between her shoulder blades.

"Do you have any idea where this problem may be coming from?" Gretchen asked the computer.

"Absolutely," the computer replied. "Hydrogen sulfide is being off-gassed by the memory machine. Any oxygen I pump into the delivery shuttle that contains it is almost immediately consumed by the machine."

"Well quit pumping oxygen in there!" Gretchen began an uncomfortable walk towards the center of the satellite.

"The quickest way to the delivery shuttle is through the ballroom and casino," the computer said. A blinking yellow arrow appeared at the edge of her heads-up display, when she looked towards it the arrow lay flat on the ground pointing towards a door. She followed it as the computer continued talking.

"According to Mr. Rungson's manuals, the memory machine needs oxygen to continue to survive, just like you. And according to Mr. Rungson's journals, it's important that I don't let this machine die."

Gretchen walked through the colorful and loud casino. Muffled jazz music echoed through her helmet.

"Do the manuals say anything about why it'd off-gas hydrogen sulfide?" she asked.

"No, he has no mention of this type of malfunction. My records do indicate that organic creatures give off hydrogen sulfide when decomposing in low oxygen environments like swamps."

"But this thing isn't in a low-oxygen environment," Gretchen said. "At least not yet." But if the computer kept feeding the delivery shuttle oxygen the whole station would be. Then the machine would suffocate and die anyway. And she'd be left with less than she started with.

She shook her head in disappointment and frustration. She immediately regretted it because the helmet went cockeyed and covered half her vision.

Readjusting the helmet Gretchen walked through the door of the ballroom. "The machine lived for centuries in space before being delivered here. It shows up and starts decomposing? What's up with that? Let's just put it back in whatever state it was in before Todd unpacked it."

"Mr. Rungson filled its stomach with enough nutrients to survive the trip. If we use the station's food reserves to feed it then we would have nothing left and it'd only hibernate for a month. Whatever Mr. Rungson was feeding it was very nutritionally dense. Plus I wouldn't be able to recover anything it ate for–"

"I don't want to hear it," Gretchen cut it off. The food tasted bad enough to her already, she didn't want to hear the details of how it was made or where it went. Her feet rubbed in unnatural places inside the large boots. She felt like a clown, in more ways than one. Who was she to think that she could fix this, escape the avians, and live on a space station like she was a part of the Galaxy Gang. She rolled her eyes at herself as she stood in front of the airlock of the delivery shuttle.

"Is there enough oxygen in there for me to breathe?" She asked. "And is there any way for you to recover the oxygen so that this station can eventually get back to habitable levels?"

"Yes, you may need to go through a few suits but there's a year's supply of oxygen in those alone."

A year inside of these potato sacks didn't sound fun. But suffocating didn't sound better. But she didn't like any of her options. Even the one she was currently leaning toward felt heartless. Like something the monster that owned this space station would do.

"Open the airlock," she commanded the computer.

"What are you going to do Mrs. Smith?"

"I'm getting the memories off that machine," she said. "Then you're going to quit giving it oxygen and we'll let it die."

16

Monika Pikowski was in hemorrhage mode. She wasn't the one hemorrhaging. The city was. Citizens were terrified and there'd be chaos in the street in no time. And to make matters worse Rungson was nowhere to be found.

She thought time travelers would be more punctual than this.

Then again he'd had a friend over. And considering there were no security records of anyone entering his mansion she had a good guess of which "friend" he was talking about.

Which didn't bode well either.

Don't trust anyone that successfully killed you. That was her rule. It was a new one. One it seemed Rungson was uneager to adopt.

The whole experience of being shot, by a laser gun no less, felt like a dream she'd woken up from and forgotten. That dreamy sensation seemed to extend to the city around her tonight. Gentle wind moved the misty night air making mirages of movement. Tonight the city was cool and crisp. Only illuminated by the street lights. Tall buildings loomed over Monika. Some brick, some printed concrete, and a few glass and iron buildings as well.

She paced back and forth across the intersection she was patrolling. No cars were out tonight. No one wanted to leave their homes... yet.

The silence of the night let her think. Let her worry. Worry about her mother, Kot, the city she was supposed to help protect. Even Rungson in some ways. To get those off her mind she thought of the problem at hand.

She was a detective. She wasn't capable of overlooking coincidences. And the fact that Rungson's killer and time-traveling monkeys appeared in the same week was a link she couldn't ignore.

Unfortunately, it was the only link she had.

Someone had killed a monkey a few hours ago. The body was in a conglomerate laboratory being dissected right now. The news was playing it up as hopeful. The enemy could be killed. It can be conquered. Everyone stay calm.

Monika didn't expect much to come from the dissection. Autopsy of a killer alien would be useful to biologists. Maybe other Central System scientists could use it to learn more. But it wouldn't help the people, 116 and counting, who were attacked in the streets and killed.

Whoever fell in the impending riots would be the worst loss of all. Deaths not by monkeys but by the chaos of fellow humans.

Which was why tonight Monika Pikowski stood on a street corner in a wind jacket with "Rungson PD" on the back, patrolling like a watchman. Every officer on the planet had been called out. There were more corners than police officers in this city. And even with all three branches of the security force called into action and the Rungson Reserve Military, there wasn't enough to keep every citizen safe.

The people in uniform knew it. And since the deaths were still rising it was only a matter of time until the citizens realized it.

Central System was sending backup. But space was big and travel through the gates was slow. They'd be here in a ten-day week. Hopefully, Monika would be too.

The mist in the empty streets didn't ruin visibility, just made the patrol work ominous. The radio mounted on Monika's shoulder rattled off various check-ins from everyone under her. She was in charge of managing the patrol in this sector of the capitol. The earpiece on her opposite side was silent but she knew it'd come to life when Stone wanted an update from her sector.

No update was a good update. She had time to think. Figure out what might be happening.

Rungson's killer wanted a ransom or something. That's why he killed Rungson. To get his attention. Were the monkeys a follow-up to that threat? Based on Rungson comparing her and every other citizen in the city to bugs, that didn't seem likely. But Rungson had been in this universe for five generations, nearly a millennium. There must be something of value to him.

Maybe that's what the alien monkeys were looking for. Some time traveler's buried treasure.

But then why did they kill so many people. And the deaths. They were terrifying. People would fight them off and then fall lifeless. The monkeys hadn't wounded anyone worse than a scratch and a bite. And after the body fell lifeless the monkeys would suddenly be interested in fighting back, swinging their long arms around in the air in mock punches, slaps, or helpless flails. Until they saw their victims were dead. Then they'd walk away from the crime disappearing into thin air.

Killing by a bite or a scratch. That made it seem like the aliens were venomous. Anything working that quickly had to be potent. Maybe the autopsy could get a sample and derive an antidote.

"Pikowski, there's one on Third and Main," an officer reported to her radio. "Three of them," he continued. "They came out of nowhere."

It was still shocking even if it's what you expected. Monika started a quick jog down the street. Her wind jacket caught the breeze she made and billowed behind her making it easy to reach the gun on her belt, she doubted she'd need any of the rest of the belt's equipment. Third was two blocks down. Main was three streets over. She hoped she could get there before the aliens disappeared, or did anything worse.

"I've got two on First and Wall," another officer reported. "Four! Elder's light," it was the voice of a different officer. Two gunshots echoed through the street. She picked up the jog to a full-out run and pulled her gun out of its holster.

"Location?" Monika asked. She rounded the sharp black brick corner of a bank and headed down Third Street.

Two monkeys stood over the body of an officer. Monika didn't know the woman. She'd come from the reserves. Volunteered to help out.

The monkeys were shorter than Monika expected. Like fifth graders who'd spent too much time at the gym and had taffy for arms. Their leathery skin was unnatural. Scales instead of hair didn't seem right on something so human-like.

The monkey that stood over the fallen officer's body had red blood around its teeth like a child that'd tried to use lipstick. Its eyes were strangely human, almost intelligent, a hazel green color. It held out its arms, its hands cupped like it was pointing a gun at her. Lucky for Monika its hands were empty.

It was the one who hadn't attacked anyone yet that Monika worried about. It rushed up to her, lumbering on its front knuckles and short back legs.

Monika fired two rounds at the ape. She hit its head. It fell to the ground. Green blood splattered across the sidewalk and street.

The enemy could be killed. It can be conquered. Stay calm Pikowski.

The lipsticked alien began its charge on two legs. She fired at it as well. Aiming at its broad chest. An easy target.

The monkey disappeared. Just like Rungson had. It could probably reappear anywhere. Just like Rungson had.

She put her back to the brick wall of the bank. If it could go through walls she had new problems. She kept an eye on the misty street.

"Officer down on Third and Emerald Ave," Monika reported into her shoulder. She flipped on her earpiece to transmit to Chief Stone. "Chief, this is Pikowski, we've got multiple sightings in my sector. At least one officer d–"

Gunshots went off in the distance and echoed through the canyon of buildings.

"Tell your sector to retreat to a dock," Stone said into her ear. His gruff voice was melancholy. Like he'd given up. "We're evacuating."

"Evacuating the whole capitol?" Monika was shocked. That was millions of people.

"The planet," Stone clarified. "We've got ships ready to launch at every dock. Get yourself there. Help others on the way. The announcement is about to go out."

The monkey with the bloody mouth appeared to her left, it cawed at her in a mock as it lumbered towards her. She fired two shots at it. They would've hit it if hadn't disappeared again.

There weren't enough ships in the whole Central System to move a planet's worth of people out. And even then. If these monkeys could travel like Rungson what's to keep them quarantined on this planet. Rungson had appeared in orbit when he died

"There will be chaos," Monika said to Stone. "There will be fighting and riots and–"

The monkey reappeared in front of her. Maybe a meter and a half away. She fired and scared it off again. She didn't have enough bullets to keep it away forever. Did the monkey know that?

"It's the only plan we've got," Stone said, resigned. "It's coming from higher up than me."

"Rungson?" Monika asked hopeful that he'd come. Even if the best he could come up with was this stupid plan. Rungson could go back in time, warn people, and start the evacuation sooner. Maybe... Then again if that was going to happen, it'd already have happened.

"Not that high," Stones said.

Monika saw the monkey appear down the street towards Main where she was headed. It cawed and screeched and pounded its chest. She noticed a crowd behind it in the mist.

The riots had begun. The people had done the math once the announcement had been made. They were in the streets. Ready to add to the chaos of the attacks.

The monkey's noises got louder, more chaotic. As the crowd stepped out of the mist she realized that the people that made it up were shorter, lankier, and not at all people.

There was a crown of alien monkeys taking up the width of the street like it was a parade.

"Stone if you haven't made that announcement don't. There are a hundred or more monkeys headed to Emerald and Third. Anyone out in the streets would–"

A roar echoed through the streets. It seemed to come from every building and every street. It was deeper than anything she ever expected from a creature so small. And it sent a shiver down Monika's spine.

17

I looked down at Dasco, his book still shut under my hand. The musky room felt cramped and small. Swee Pip ruffled her jet black wings seemingly nervous by my looming threat. My eyebrows were tight. I felt fury burning behind my eyes.

And Dasco looked up at me as composed as the suit and bowler hat he wore. If there was rage in his previous statement about being upset that I hadn't shared the memory-wiping technology with him it was tied up tight like his black necktie. Dasco took a measured breath, let it out, and then gestured to a high-backed burgundy chair that hadn't been there before.

"Sit," Dasco said. It was an offer as much as a command.

I leaned against the arm in a way that would frustrate my mother, and hopefully Dasco too. I was in no mood to be comfortable.

"Have you forgotten I'm dying?" He asked.

Swee Pip whistled a slow deep whistle. It felt like an uncouth reaction to the announcement. She'd perched herself and a rod. Her wings were stretched out to her sides making her look like a mountain.

"I've forgotten everything," I said, frustrated that I'd had to repeat myself so many times. Plus the admission was uncomfortable. Hard to grasp. There were spots of my past that Woah Te had brought up in the Mother Tree. A connection to life that seemed to fade if I didn't nurture it. And it was as difficult to nurture as a toddler who doesn't want to eat their greens.

"We're immortal," I added. Hesitant to be tricked by Dasco's statement, if I was supposed to feel something for Dasco's death I didn't. Clearly, he was trying to play on my emotions. "I've tried dying a dozen ways since I learned I could survive death the first time under the wheels of that SUV."

Swee Pip clicked her beak, like chattering teeth. Dasco straightened his suit jacket in the wooden chair. My wooden chair.

"We're as immortal as a teapot," Dasco said. "We don't break down, but if we get too full then what use are we?"

Always with the tea. "And I poured out my memories because I was too full?" I asked

"You, me, Swee Pip, we all face the same problem. The last time I saw Gretchen she was scouring the mother tree for answers. She was just as obsessed as you'd been. Although you apparently found it: a way to lose our mind."

"She said she wanted her memory wiped to get rid of an avian tracking device," I said.

Dasco nodded. "She seemed to have fixed that ages ago. I'm glad you helped me avoid that fiasco."

I shook my head. A whole gang of time travelers. Who could keep their own timeline straight? Let alone their friend's. "I had to have a reason to keep it from myself. Wipe the device out of my memory. If I knew where it was in the multiverse I could take you there."

Sometimes I could be an asshole, but if Dasco was really my friend why would I want to hide this from him? Which meant either he wasn't my friend or it wasn't ready for others to use. My lack of useful memories might be evidence of that.

"Maybe a simpler question," I said. Frustrated by the tautology of the situation. "Where'd the chairs come from?"

Dasco laughed. Swee Pip chipped a few whistles. "That's not significantly simpler," he said. "I summoned them or imagined and created them. You know how in your dreams things appear when you think about them? It's what I did here." Dasco took a deep breath and a steaming porcelain tea cup appeared next to the books.

"I don't dream, haven't in a while," I said. It was mostly true, except for the time I'd been trapped in Gretchen's universe without my powers. But I didn't feel like confusing the situation.

"No, we don't dream," Dasco said, almost longingly. "Dreaming is the conscious body exploring without the guidance of our physical body. When you can fully control your conscious body and roam the multiverse it has no need to wander out at night."

"So I could just go back to my office and summon a pile of gold?" It really undermined the generations I spent building up the Rungson Conglomerate.

"No, you can't. Right now we're not in the multiverse. We're on an astral plane. This is where some dreams take place, ones where you're exploring your subconscious, resolving the stresses of the day. Your conscious body can build a nest here based on your memories. I just did it... more intentionally."

"Which is why I can't travel out of it? Why we need the necklaces."

"No." Dasco smiled.

I groaned and slumped into the high back chair frustrated.

"I told you this wasn't significantly simpler. The Mother Tree is in the astral plane, we can travel in and out of that without a problem." He looked towards the domed ceiling of the observatory as an additional thought came to him. "Well, the avians are a bit of a problem, but not the same kind."

"What's their deal?" I asked.

"One question at a time," Dasco continued. "This pearlescent city I've built has insulation around it to make it difficult for people to find and enter. But if you know where to look you can slip in."

"City? I've only seen two rooms."

"Yes, I know. It's a shame you forgot how nice it is, really undermines my hard work. Especially since when I die it will disappear, along with these habitats." Dasco gestured to the observatory around him.

"Why's it disappearing?" I asked.

"I created them, from my memory. They're an extension of my mind and conscious body. Once I die..." he made an exploding motion with his fingers.

"Tooodd is becoming confused. You're mixing metaphors," Swee Pip interjected.

She was right. "If we were teapots then this city would have nowhere it needed to go, you just wouldn't be able to make new memories," I said. Although that in and of itself was a head-scratcher.

"The memories aren't killing me," Dasco said. He tapped his right knee, the one he seemed to avoid in favor of the cane. "A parasite is.

"They got in a few lifetimes ago. Funny, I collect so many creatures and now I've got a few million as a pet in my knee. And even if I exterminate everyone they find a way back. And I think it's something in my memories that's helping them hone in on me."

"But they're affecting your physical body. Those regenerate if we die." Hell, I'd killed him only a few days ago and now he was sitting here in front of me.

"They're in my conscious body. I just isolate them in my knee by imagining I have pain there. But they get out occasionally and I reduce them back with a holly-lopper who likes to eat them. But they're escaping my knee quicker and quicker these days. Eventually, they'll chew me up completely, erode the city, and my mind."

"Which is why it'll disappear even if your memories don't," I said finally catching on. "Whatever I used did a number on my memory as well. Maybe I tried to use a similar parasite."

"Unlikely," Dasco said. "You're more cautious than me around these kinds of creatures. You'd sooner shepherd eons of evolution before trusting something nature concocted. Which is why you never helped me with the garmound."

"And why do you need the garmound? Does its drool work as an ointment to help your knee?"

Dasco flipped back and opened the book I'd shut. He skimmed through a couple pages and eventually found the one he was looking for because he held it up to show me like a school librarian.

A sketch of a small puppy took up the majority of the page. Strange curved symbols surrounded it marking out the anatomy of the the thing. It was not a normal puppy. Despite its mouth being closed it was clear the beast was still a garmound, it had tentacles reaching out of its shoulders. Additionally, something I hadn't noticed when facing the beast in real life was that it didn't have ears like a dog either. Which added to the sharp cone shape of its face. Instead, there were craters on the side of its skull which seemed to let in sound. Reminded me of a bigger version of lizard ears.

"The pups of the garmound are less dangerous. A full-grown one will devour your conscious body in a moment and can hunt you down across the multiverse with its senses. But we could capture a puppy and hold it here in the pearlescent city without a problem."

"Your dying wish is to have a pet that could kill you once it's fully grown?"

"The mother, unsurprisingly won't be too happy. She'll be willing to track the pup anywhere we take it. And we could use it as bait to lead her to your world where the lefths are invading."

"Speaking of evading you haven't clarified why you want it." I was beginning to worry he had nefarious intentions, and as scary as the full-grown one was the puppy was pretty cute and I'd hate for anything bad to happen to it.

"Garmounds have incredible control of their conscious body," Dasco said. "More control than you, me, or any avian. We, humans, can reach out and find our way through the multiverse with enough focus and practice and some help connecting the dots across our default lives. Avians seem to pick it up easier migrating to the Mother Tree naturally once their mind develops enough."

"We believe it's because of the amount of time we spend in the egg," Swee Pip interjected sounding proud of her species' evolutionary accomplishment.

"Garmounds can not only travel through the multiverse they can sense things in it. You and I feel it out with our breath and mind. These beasts smell, hear, see the branches of time stretch out in front of them. Even as puppies.

"And if I had a puppy I could hunt you down through the multiverse and find out where your memory machine is hidden."

18

I looked down at the nest full of pups. They were curled into balls and squished against each other in a bedding of leaves and tall matted grass. The grass was shockingly green and coiled tightly. The leaves were large fern-like branches. I hadn't seen a tree last time I was on the planet. Who knows where the garmound mother dragged that bedding in from.

I had a necklace hanging around my neck. Different from the wooden coin and the crystal. This one was a green figurine of a mermaid woman. Her arms were extended and looped through the black cordage.

It was supposed to take me back to Griffith. After I snagged one of the pups out of this damp cave.

All the pups in the nest waved their tentacles aimlessly in the air. None of them were bigger than a volleyball. Most of them slept. One poked her head out of the nest and looked at me. Her eyes were like radiant emeralds with wide black pupils in the center. She yawned at me, and she seemed as good a choice as any of the other pups in the pile.

I scooped her up, waking a few of her siblings in the process. Their tentacles reached out for my hand but after feeling me they let go.

Indifferent to the abduction of their sister. I planned to bring her back, just needed her help with something.

The pup in my arms, wrapped the tentacles of her hips and shoulders around my forearm and bicep to help stabilize herself. The pup looked at my other arm which was moving to grab the necklace.

She unhinged her jaws on both axes and latched onto my forearm with her needle-like teeth.

It stung like I'd stepped on a Lego but based on how dangerous Swee Pip and Dasco made her mother out to be the pup's bite didn't hurt me as much as I expected. Something tingled inside my arm. I shook her off and she let go. But only to reposition herself to bite me again.

I grabbed the mermaid around my neck and gray static filled my peripherals. The pup let go, of her own free will this time. She let out a little roar that sounded more like a goose-honking than a ferocious beast.

Tightening her grip on my arm with her tentacles I felt the floor drop out from beneath me. Unfazed by the fall through time and space the puppy began to nibble on the hand I had wrapped around her chest to hold her in place. She couldn't get a good angle to bite me despite being able to unhinge her jaw, and I was glad there was something to keep her distracted.

I landed in a storage room I didn't recognize. Crates labeled with various foodcrowave meals lined the wire shelves on the walls. The opposite side had tools for cleaning and gardening along with a couple yellow tool chests.

Dasco leaned on his cobra cane in the same nice suit he'd been wearing lately. Swee Pip stood behind him her wings folded close to her back since they would nearly brush the ceiling of the storage room if she extended them.

"We should hurry," Dasco said. He led the way to a door of the room. He took uneven steps and the metal tip of the cane echoed through the cavernous room.

We stepped out into a kitchen that felt familiar, if only because it used the same white marble that was abundant on Griffith. Then we stepped into the living room of the house. An abstract statue that looked like a melted snowman gave me my bearings.

"Do you have a car we can use?" Dasco said.

The puppy in my arms had gotten bored of trying to gnaw on my hand and moved her tentacles up my arm and around my shoulder crawling up my body to explore other options to perch on. Her claws dug into my skin but the thick leather of my jacket protected me for the most part. Unfortunately, the jacket was scratched beyond repair by the time she found a cozy spot on my shoulder.

"Probably," I said. "I could get a driver here in five minutes or less."

Swee Pip began to extend her wings as we walked into the high-ceiling foyer. She flapped up to the second story and looked down at us. "I don't think we have that lo–"

A roar cut her off and Dasco grabbed my hand his cane clattering to the marbled floor. He took a deep breath and we were in the streets of Griffith's capitol city. A mist had rolled in at some point giving the lamp-lit streets an eerie glow.

It was crisp. The back of my neck and cheeks felt a chill. The pup nuzzled up next to me her fur was warm even if it was a little sharp like two-day-old stubble.

Swee Pip swooped into the canyon-like street. As she folded her wings back mist cleared around her. "There's a flock of the lefths a little north of here," she said.

"Is the mother going to be distracted enough by them to leave us alone?" I asked.

The pup on my shoulder let out a delayed squawk of a roar which was only uncomfortable because of how close she was to my ear, which she began to nibble on. I cocked my head to get my ear away from her.

A headache began on that side of my head. This was no time to be dealing with a migraine.

"She will if we don't give her an easy trail," Dasco said handing me a crystal necklace he produced from inside his suit jacket.

I grabbed it by the cord being careful to keep the crystal away from my skin and lowered it around my neck. We made our way north with Swee Pip flying from building to building and me jogging to keep up with her. Dasco kept up with us by taking focused breaths and appearing at the end of the street.

The streets were empty, which was strange even though it was late at night. Usually, a city as populated as this would have a few people out and about. But a curfew or shelter-in-place order must have gone into effect to keep everyone inside.

The garmound pup stood firmly on the scratched-up shoulder of my jacket. She occasionally tightened her tentacle grip around my arm when I took a turn quickly or took a big step over a curb. Running in boots wasn't easy. I was glad I could trust the pup to hold herself in place.

I rounded the corner of a black-bricked building and found a woman lying dead on the sidewalk she wore a windbreaker with "Rungson PD" on the back. The fact she was the first police person I'd seen tonight was concerning.

Dasco appeared next to me, he sounded almost as out of breath as I was. Traveling like that must've been exhausting in its own way.

The woman had drawn her gun, but bite marks on her neck made it clear that the lefth that'd attacked her had gotten to her first. I wondered if bullets could even hurt the lefths as I picked up the woman's gun and checked that it was still loaded. Better safe than sorry.

I noticed Swee Pip swooping down from the building she'd perched on. But she was the least of my worries. At the end of the street, I saw Pikowski talking to someone. The flock of lefths that Swee Pip mentioned was just past her in the mist.

The pup on my shoulder let out a little growl at the crowd of beasts. But it was overshadowed by the deafening roar of her mother.

"This is close enough," Dasco said. "Let's go."

"What's the garmound going to do to Pikowski? The city buildings? The other citizens?" It wasn't the first time I'd thought of the concern but it was the first time I'd voiced it.

"She could kill everyone in this city and it'd be less destruction than a lefth invasion," Dasco said. "Give me the pup and I'll go myself. It's got your scent by now."

Dasco reached for the puppy on my shoulder. I was willing to let him have her and shrugged towards him. The puppy had other plans. Her tentacles held tight to my arm and one wrapped around my neck to keep her in place. Dasco was a little more stubborn than her. Until she bit his hand.

He gave me a glare, his icy blue eyes were set in a betrayed scowl. I shrugged, not much I could do to convince the pup to leave me, and besides I was the one being choked by her tentacles.

A second roar put an end to our silent argument. Dasco clutched the crystal around his neck and disappeared.

I should've done the same. But Pikowski stood in the middle of the street terrified and just now noticing me. I had to get at least her to safety. Even if safety was Dasco's Pearlescent City.

But it was too late for any of that. The garmound mother was bounding down the street headed straight for me and her daughter.

19

The garmound mother stared me down as she ran towards me. She took up the entire car lane and her sharp nose looked like a fighter jet. It felt like she was moving almost as fast as one.

Which made my gut reaction pretty dumb. But that's why it's a gut reaction, not a brain reaction.

I ran away from her. Towards Pikowski and the horde of lefths that took up the width of the street.

I got to Pikowski before the garmound did but only by a hair. I grabbed her arm dragging her with me. She caught on quick enough and wore more sensible shoes. She easily kept pace with me.

The garmound pup sat between us on my shoulder, still wrapping her tentacle around my neck. Luckily she was no longer choking me, it was hard enough to breathe while running. The lefth horde in front of us was only a little further away than the garmound mother who I thought I could feel breathing down my neck.

I took a deep breath, not easy while running, and reached out for somewhere past the mist. My aim was haphazard, risky, dangerous. I'd survive appearing in the wall of a building. But I wasn't confident Pikowski or the pup would. However, I was confident if I didn't do anything we wouldn't survive the crowd of lefths we were headed for.

I exhaled as the lefth at the front of the crowd, red blood around its lips, leaped out at me.

I stumbled to the ground. Pikowski fell with me. The pup landed on her feet with a little squawk of a roar, her black fur almost blended in with the asphalt of the street.

I scrambled to my feet and pointed the gun that was still in my hand at the lefth that would surely be on top of me.

It wasn't. The crowd was behind me.

I'd made the jump, somehow with the gun still in my hand, my jacket was the same, but still had scratches from the pup's journey up my arm back at the mansion.

Something abnormal was happening but I didn't have time to work it out.

"What in the name of the Elders is going on?" Pikowski said scrambling up from the ground.

Swee Pip landed next to us almost invisible in the dark night. The horde stood between the garmound mother and us, for now. Her pup was pawing at my calf, obviously wanting back up to her high vantage point on my shoulder.

"That thing should take care of the lefths," I told Pikowski, just now realizing how much faith I'd put into Dasco, a man I hadn't known nearly long enough.

The garmound mother ran into the crowd of lefths like a bowling ball. The crowd scattered, not by running but by flashing in and out of existence. A few dozen teleported to her back but were slung off by her tentacles. She bit at a few not bothering to unhinge her jaw in the vertical axis.

The mother continued to make her way towards me. The white light of the street lamps shone off her dark green eyes and she looked fiercely determined to get the pup that sat on my shoulder. And at the rate she was going it wouldn't take her long to get rid of the lefths attacking her.

I hadn't put the puppy on my shoulder, and I certainly would've noticed her climbing up my jeans and scratched jacket. But nonetheless, she was there perched next to me growling and barking at the lefths that were attacking her mother.

"They're multiplying," Pikowski pointed out. And she was right there were far more lefths in front of the garmound than just the original crowd. The tide of the lefth's recently hopeless fight seemed to be turning.

"They're bringing in reinforcements," Swee Pip replied. And, ever the professional, Pikowski didn't even appear bothered by a talking bird.

The pup leapt off my shoulder and in midair disappeared only to reappear a few feet in front of me on the ground. It was running towards its mother interested in somehow helping.

If the pup and mother reunited then all this would be for naught. I chased after the little garmound as she let out little barks at the lefths that towered over her.

A half dozen lefths had noticed the yapping pup coming towards them and began circling her. I held the gun out in front of me and shot at two, taking them down without a problem.

That drew the remaining lefth's attention away from the ankle-tall puppy and onto me. A real meal.

The remaining four ran towards me. A gunshot came from behind me and slowed one of them down. Then the other three disappeared.

They instantly reappeared inches from my face.

Their long limbs had wrapped themselves around my outstretched arms and legs before I knew what was happening.

Sharp claws cut through the sleeves of my jacket shredding it to pieces, and slicing into the flesh of my right forearm. I shouted in pain inches from the lefth's elongated scaly snouts.

The monkeys reacted with hisses of their own. They lifted up their lips like a horse would and exposed long white fangs and breath that reeked of rotten meat.

The pup was suddenly at my eye level, perched on the shoulder of a lefth that was about to sink its teeth into my shoulder.

Her jaw opened as wide as it could go in all four directions, exposing the pink gums of her mouth. Her two worm-like tongues shot out of the back of her throat trying to claw under its tight scales. She bit into the lefth's throat her emerald eyes were small but ferocious.

Her bite distracted the lefth and freed my arm. I pointed my gun at one of the two remaining lefths that were on me. I shot it a few times in its broad chest and the gunshot was deafening. Green blood splattered all over me and the street.

There was still one next to me. Its face was close to mine. I had no doubt it wanted to rip the flesh off my skull.

Three yellow talons embedded themselves into the lefth's face. Adding more green blood to the mess that covered my body and now face. Using her massive wings to give her power Swee Pip hurled the lefth across the street and into the second-story window of a hopefully vacant bank.

"It's time to go Tooodd," Swee Pip said. She pulled the cord of a necklace out of the purple sash that hung around her chest.

She was right. As much damage as the garmound mother would do to the city having her puppy here to reunite with her would leave an army of lefths and nothing strong enough to stop them.

I scooped up the pup that was gnawing on the neck of the limp lefth she'd taken down. Her teeth didn't seem to cut through the beast's scales but whatever she'd done had immobilized the lefth. And the size difference was even more terrifying than watching the lefth attack for the first time.

There was one Griffith citizen I could keep safe from the lefths and garmound. Pikowski was a few yards away shooting at a few more lefths that were approaching us.

The garmound mother, now covered in lefths, roared and shook them off her back. She looked like a dog trying to get dry in a rainstorm. And it seemed just about as effective.

I ran for Pikowski who was hastily reloading her pistol as two lefths ran towards her. I linked my arm under hers as she slammed the clip into the bottom of her gun.

With my bloody free hand, I grabbed the crystal of my necklace.

20

My face lay on the cream floor. Its pink and purple sheen glistened in the white light that filled the room. It smelled like a fishmonger's cutting board.

I shouted in pain. It felt like my entire being was leaking out of my right arm. And the departure of that being was as uncomfortable as stopping a bullet with my chest.

Someone rolled me over. Something was wrong, horribly wrong. I stopped screaming, but only because it felt rude to do it right in Pikowski's face.

My right arm was bleeding. My jacket was ripped to shreds. I clutched my arm but it only covered my left hand in blood. Green blood from the lefths was mixed in and had a more sticky saliva-like texture.

I groaned to stifle another scream. It felt like I was giving birth to something out of my forearm. And whatever was leaving me felt the need to drag parts of me out with it.

I'd died multiple times. Often painfully. Occasionally pointlessly. I was not used to having to deal with the consequences of that pain after traveling across the multiverse.

Pikowski squatted next to me. The garmound pup had begun to lick my wounds with her strange worm-like tongues. It didn't take long to realize we were at the beginning of Dasco's maze.

The bastard couldn't drop us closer to him? I'd bleed out before I could solve this thing. Why'd he take his security so seriously? It was an inconvenience to everyone.

Pikowski was standing over me. Her hands had blue gloves on them, although those were beginning to be covered in red and green blood. She had a tight vest and collared button-up shirt on, instead of the Rungson PD windbreaker. She pulled something out of her police utility belt and wrapped it around my bicep.

"That'll stop you from bleeding out," she said. "but you'll lose your arm if we don't get medical help soon."

"Dasco!" I cried out in frustration and pain. Maybe the call would summon him, have him take down this stupid maze. There was some information I was missing and I had no doubt that he was orchestrating it.

"Relax," Pikowski said lifting my less bloody arm over her shoulder. "You've already died twice since I met you."

I groaned in pain. Her levity should've given me a chuckle. Maybe a retort of my own. But something was truly wrong with my forearm.

Pikowski reached the hand that wasn't carrying me out to follow the wall. When she turned to follow it the garmound pup barked at us.

Pikowski jumped at the sound and it jarred my arm. I shouted in pain but neither of the ladies cared. They were more focused on getting me out. The pup walked away from us her conical nose close to the ground.

"Trust the dog," I said. I began to move in the direction of the pup but it hurt to put weight on my left leg.

I looked down and there was a massive gash in my thigh. My jeans were soaked in blood. The lefths must have gotten to that too.

"You were covered in them," Pikowski said as she led me down the maze behind the pup. "I would've shot them off you but I didn't want to hurt you or the raven."

"At least if you shot me I probably wouldn't be in this much pain," I said. The pup led us around some invisible turns. And I could see what Dasco meant when he talked about garmounds having incredible control of their senses.

"What's going on?" Pikowski asked. Her tone was serious and professional. I was still haunted by the wounds of the lefths but she'd somehow seemed to put it to the back of her mind. Interested in uncovering more answers.

"The big four-legged dog thing, it's called a garmound. I stole her pup. Used the pup to lure her to Griffith so she would take care of the lefths. Lefth is what Dasco calls the lizard-monkeys."

"And Dasco is your killer friend?"

"Yes. And Swee Pip is the bird," I was too tired to do the popping sound with my lips as I said her name. "That garamond will be following me through the multiverse until she gets her puppy back."

Pikowski looked behind us and the sudden shift hurt my back. Was there a cut there too? Being mortal sucks.

"This place is insulated. Don't ask me how or what that means, I don't know." I could see the edge of the maze. From my time going through it with Dasco, I knew it meant we were a little over halfway through.

"Is your friend Dasco going to kill me again?" Pikowski asked. It wasn't an accusation and she didn't sound frustrated. Just curious. Trying to be prepared.

"I hope not," I said. "But if he does and you wind up back on Griffith, and if Griffith isn't a pile of lefth-infested rubble I need you to send off some files."

With the pain I was in and the fact that my powers hadn't been working quite right since I started chasing down the lefths on Griffith I was feeling my mortality. And with that came despair. I'd lived a long enough life to forget most of it. But I still felt like I had unfinished business.

"How am I going–"

"I don't care. Break into my mansion if you have to. Get a subpoena or whatever bureaucratic bullshit you need to. There are two files on my office terminal. One's an order for clothes and station supplies and another is a text file with important specs on it. Send them Gretchen Smith who lives on a satellite I commissioned called Fortress of Solitude. Parameters for that are on the same terminal."

"Do you have a password? Encryption? There's got to be a dozen security things I can't get past without you."

The pup led us to the long hallway with the aperture doorway at the end of it. Behind us, a trail of my blood showed the perfect solution to the maze. As neat as that was, I wished it was still in my body because I was feeling lightheaded.

"I'm immortal," was immortal, "I don't really worry about security like that. Because it's more of a hindrance than a help." I said the last sentence as loud as I could so Dasco could hear my disdain for his maze.

"You're insane. You'll be fine." Pikowski tried to sound lighthearted but I could hear concern in her voice.

The muscles of the ornate circular doorway opened up and Pikowski helped me into the domed room filled with zoo enclosures.

Something roared in the distance. Maybe a beast in an enclosure. Maybe something worse. I was in too much pain to care.

I hoped Pikowski was right, hoped I was insane, and would be fine. Most of all I hoped the pup could lead her to Dasco, who should've greeted us by now.

He was probably drinking tea in his parlor, bulbous laser gun ready to put me out of my misery.

The bright pearlescent room faded black as I closed my eyes.

Unfortunately, it seemed like something had beat him to it.

21

Gretchen sat in the reclined chair of the memory machine. It reminded her of something she'd find in a gym's weight room. But it was far from the worst thing about the machine. The only thing making the chair comfortable was the fact the room had no gravity. Her boots connected her to the ground.

The memory machine looked as horrid as it did when Todd first unpacked it. Metal racks were covered in veins like messy wires from one of her Todd's computer projects. The purple heart was the largest organ but others were hanging inside the racks. Each was a dark green, blue, or purple color. Alien and inhuman. Some organs glistened with slime, others were soft and flexed as fluid pumped through them. A few looked like they had blisters and boils growing on them. She hoped that wasn't new but had a feeling it was part of the reason the machine was off-gassing hydrogen sulfide.

A few traditional wires ran from the computer terminal and keyboard to the machine. But after a yard of wire, they were spliced open and connected, more like infused, with the veins of the machine.

A plastic face mask rested around her nose and chin. It fed her oxygen from the green metal tank that sat next to her. The gas was cool, sterile, but still let in a bit of sewage stench.

The bulky space suit still covered the rest of her body but she couldn't connect to the memory machine with a helmet on. To keep from suffocating on hydrogen sulfide she had to get an oxygen tank out of the medbay.

Now she sat reclined, but not relaxed. The purple heart behind her beat slowly. The closing and opening of valves seemed to echo through the delivery shuttle. She didn't want the thing to die. She wanted Todd to be here to help her. Either Todd would do. She wasn't picky at this point.

She didn't want to stick the monster's memories into her head. He'd haunted her nightmares for what felt like lifetimes. She was willing to work with him and forgive him. But memories inside her, that was too intimate.

Unfortunately, she had no choice. The computer would kill her before letting the machine die and losing Todd's memories. As far as it knew she was immortal, the machine was not.

She twisted the computer screen to face her. She could barely reach the keyboard. It was clearly designed to be used by two people: a doctor and a patient. The keyboard itself was a strange design that started with QWE instead of the expected ZPX she was used to. Electronics always had weird mutations across the multiverse.

The screen lit up after she pressed the blank space bar a few times. It was a simple green text on a black background. Rudimentary. No more complicated than it needed to be. According to the satellite's computer, who'd read Todd's manuals, the organs would do most of the work.

The screen displayed a file system. Three files were there. Only labeled with numbers. Apparently, Todd didn't see the need to be specific with the labeling. Seemed dumb and careless. But that was typical of this version of him.

Gods only knew what she was about to put in her head.

With a deep breath, she selected memory number one and sat back in the chair.

Veins that grew around the metal of the machine reached up over the chair and wrapped themselves around her forehead like a sweat-band. They weaved under her plastic oxygen mask letting the strong stench of hydrogen sulfide in. Unfortunately, the smell was instantly muted by the veins wriggling their way into her nostrils.

She wanted to sit up. Get out of the chair. Rip the veins off.

Orbiting Jupiter for an eternity would be better than this!

She stood in a field. Green rolling hills reached out to the horizon. The sky was purple and the ground was soft. The air smelled like freshly cut flowers and it was a pleasant improvement over the hydrogen sulfide.

Coiled grass covered the ground. She stood on large stones that sat just above the grass sinking in like a heavy weight on a pillow-top bed.

She followed the path. She didn't want to but she did. She wasn't in control. Like she was in a dream. She saw the world around her but couldn't interact.

Black square buildings dotted the hills around her. People moved about from building to building. They walked with strange gaits like they were just about to fall over any minute.

The path led her down the hill and to a large workshop. Big doors hung on rails and rolled open and closed. The roof was a single pitch, made with corrugated metal. It looked like a ramp launching into the purple sky. The siding was ribbed concrete like someone had iced a cake but never smoothed it out.

She walked inside, the ground was dirt here the coiled grass had stopped a few yards from the entrance.

A person hobbled up to her. He looked two-dimensional, like a gingerbread man. Unlike a gingerbread man his head was square and so were his arms which split into three fingers and an opposable thumb.

His limbs were flexible, almost boneless. If she hadn't just looked at the memory machine it would've disgusted her. Just like the people she saw in the distance, he walked like he'd fall over any moment.

His face had a human mouth and eyes. Both seemed too big for his face giving him cartoonish proportions. He had no nose. His body was flat and textureless, smooth like a baby. His skin, she didn't have a better way to describe it, was crayon blue.

"Ready for your test Mr. Rungson?" the person asked.

"Ready as I'll ever be," Gretchen said. Her voice was not her own. It was deeper. But it didn't quite sound like Todd's, a voice she should've been familiar with.

"You wanted a mirror," The flexible man produced a polished metal mirror that looked closer to a frying pan than anything she'd see at a salon. She held it up and looked at herself in it. She had Todd's face. He had a thick, but not particularly long, beard with streaks of grey in it. His messy hair had matching streaks.

"If this works you should be experiencing this memory as if it was your own," Todd said into the mirror. To Gretchen, it felt like he was talking directly to her. "There are a hundred things I need to communicate to you, Dasco. And text files won't do it all justice."

Todd smiled. Gretchen felt her lips do it but she wanted to crinkle her nose and gag in disgust. She felt like a bird in a cage. A puppet on strings.

Something stood in the corner of her eye. It wasn't another flexible man. It was a real and rigid human. Although they looked old, scrappy, and hunched over by time.

Todd didn't look in that direction so she couldn't get a better look. Instead, he headed towards the memory machine which sat on the dirt floor. The purple heart was a bit smaller and beat a little quicker. But other than that the veins still wrapped around the computer screen and metal posts.

Todd took a seat in the inclined chair. The scrappy man walked up to her. It was an old and decrepit version of Todd with leathery skin that was baggier than the space suit she'd worn. He had long white hair and an equally long and white beard. Both were patchy as if he'd pulled it out in places. He loomed over Gretchen and she could, unfortunately, see he was missing most of his teeth and his lips were dried and chapped.

Todd, the one who controlled her body didn't acknowledge the older version of himself. Gretchen wanted to scream but her body just recited specifications to the flexible lab assistant.

The scrappy man grabbed Gretchen's face. She could feel his hands on her. Yet her body didn't react. She wanted to claw him off. Push him back. It wouldn't be hard.

It felt like his fingers reached past her skin. She felt veins wrap around her forehead, up her nose. The scrappy man dug around inside her head like he was squeezing a lemon dry.

Gretchen screamed. She sat up, not far to go in the inclined chair. She heard the snap of veins and didn't care.

A heartbeat raced and it sounded louder than before, faster. She realized it was hers, not the purple one behind her.

She felt her hair. It floated behind her tied in a ponytail. There was no one grabbing her face anymore. She was grateful to the gods to be in control of her body once again.

She had experienced what she thought would be impossible.

She had met a more monstrous version of Todd Rungson.

22

Monika's shoulder was weighed down by Rungson's limp body. His breath was faint. Only audible over the sounds of the strange wildlife around her because it was so close to her ear.

Her blue gloves made her hands clammy, but she was used to the sensation from spending long hours in them while surveying crime scenes. Her vest and shirt were covered in Rungson's blood and some of the green blood from the lefths. She'd be disappointed they were ruined if they were the real thing.

The little garmound weaved through the numerous animal exhibits that filled this domed room. The puppy seemed to know what she was doing. Monika never considered herself a dog person but she was glad not to be alone now that Rungson had passed out.

The tourniquet she put on Rungson would only do him so much good. He had seemed worried. Asked her to do strange and illegal things if he died. Even if she was being ordered by the head of the conglomerate it still felt wrong to break into his personal files.

That was a problem for another day. The current issue was getting him help. Did the dog know that? She seemed dead set on whatever path she was following. She hadn't looked up since they got here, her conical face was continually pressed to the ground.

What the pup smelled was a mystery to Monika. All she could make out was the strange fishy odor. Even walking near the pen of a giant elephant-like creature she expected to be able to smell it and the swampy environment that surrounded it.

But no. There was no swampy smell. Just fish. Monika hatted fish. Although she was used to it. Kot's favorite meal was imitation salmon. And he demanded it often and unrelentingly.

She hoped her mother was able to go by and check on him. She hoped her mother was still alright, along with everyone else on Griffith. Kot might be able to keep her safe from a lefth attack. But more than likely the two would find somewhere to hide together. Kot was good at hiding without being seen.

A whistle broke Monika out of her reverie and the garmound pup picked up her pace weaving through the various environments around them. Monika dragged Rungson as best she could. She was glad she had stuck with her PT training despite becoming a detective. Other detectives let it lapse and would've been useless in moments like these.

Then again those same detectives probably wouldn't get dragged into ridiculous situations like this.

Wouldn't that be nice?

In a jungle exhibit, she saw the black-winged raven standing over the killer, Dasco. Dasco was sitting on a stool-sized mushroom. He wore a white collared shirt stained with sweat. One sleeve was rolled up and pitcher plant had swallowed his hand up to his forearm. The rest of his suit was lying on the grassy ground with a bowler hat on top.

The garmound pup rushed towards the pair. Monika hoped one of the two humanoids could help her with Rungson's body.

The pup jumped over the small mound and into the jungle. She looked around, the pair looked towards Monika and she waved and shouted for help with the body. Both looked in her direction but didn't make eye contact.

She slowly dragged Rungson and eventually made it to the jungle exhibit. She stepped over the mound. She expected it to be difficult since she was used to it demarcating an invisible wall. Instead, it was as simple as stepping over a curb.

The pair of humanoids finally looked at her and more importantly Rungson's limp body. The garmound ran between Rungson and the bird barking and yapping incessantly. She remembered why she wasn't a dog person.

She also realized why the humanoids couldn't see her.

She was now surrounded by lush green jungle, a dense canopy of leaves hung above her. Thick trees and undergrowth surrounded her in all directions. The pearlescent room she'd just left had disappeared.

Animals chirped incessantly like a crowd leaving a club after last call. However, the sounds ranged from quick chirps to rattles and cawing that made her worried a lefth would jump out from behind any bush. After all, monkeys did live in jungles.

"Rungson's bleeding," Monika said, she was worried and because of that was stating the obvious and useless things. But no one had shot her with a laser gun yet so that was an improvement. "He appeared like this even though he traveled. The lefths attacked him. Scratched up his arm."

"He should've healed upon his return," Dasco said. His arm was covered in an oblong pitcher plant with neon blue spots.

"He traveled with the garmound," the bird, Swee Pip, said. "The pup will leave his possessions in place," she continued.

She moved towards Rungson and lifted him off Monika's shoulders. She carefully lay him on the long straight grass of the forest floor.

Her yellow talon hands inspected the tourniquet that Monika had fastened to Rungson's bicep.

Monika's neck was wet with sweat. The hot and damp air around her kept her sweat on her skin and she missed the crisp cool air of the capital city. Even if it was being infested with violent lizard monkeys right now.

"Would the garmound make him keep the wounds?" Monika asked. She could hear the desperate worry in her voice and hated that it showed so clearly. "He said he could heal. That he was immortal."

"He may have over-exaggerated that claim," Dasco said. And Monika wondered what kind of friend he was to Rungson if he didn't even move to help.

"You've seen the lefths kill," Swee Pip let out a whistle that when up and back down in pitch. She looked up at Monika, her yellow eyes were waiting for an answer.

"Yes, I have. Their venom works quickly."

"They aren't venomous. They kill their victims by feeding on their consciousness." Swee Pip's voice was airy and singsong. Monika thought the sound would be beautiful if she wasn't sharing such terrifying information.

"Which is why the lefths act like their victims and fight back." Once she had all the right clues she'd come to the right conclusions.

Swee Pip whistled as she stood up. Monika assumed it was an approval. Her wings made her look massive, even though her sleek black head was only a few centimeters higher than Monika's.

"Their scratches have damaged his conscious body. And it's showing through his wounds," Swee Pip said. She left Rungson lying on the ground, his wounds were clotting but still looked awful.

With a few flaps of her wings, Swee Pip launched off the ground and flew off between some large jungle trees.

The garmound pup had found a way to curl up in Rungson's armpit. It'd be cute if she wasn't using her two wormy tongues to lick the scratches on his arm.

The lefths were so dangerous that Monika couldn't even understand what Swee Pip meant by attacking a consciousness. Psychic warfare? Like a fantasy movie? All of Griffith would've been wiped out if Rungson hadn't been there to help them out.

Assuming the garmound mother took care of the problem. And didn't knock down every building in the capitol in the process.

Monika would've considered it luck that lefths attacked a city where an immortal multiverse traveler called home. But she was a detective and simple explanations like luck didn't suffice.

A whistle came from above as Swee Pip swooped back down onto the clearing. She had a dozen bright green leaves in her hands each one the size of one of her wings.

She began laying them on the ground next to Rungson and wrapping his arm up in them.

"How did the lefth's and the garmound find Griffith?" Monika asked.

Swee Pip gave her an explanation about how lefths look for conscious beings through the multiverse. She said all this as she worked on Rungson but Monika watched Dasco who sat on the toadstool immobile and silent. She'd talked to enough guilty criminals to tell his ice-blue eyes were hiding something.

"What are the odds that they found Rungson's home though?" Monika wasn't great at math, there were statisticians and data scientists who worked for the department and handled that stuff. But she didn't need to be good to know the odds were low.

"In an infinite universe anything is possible," Dasco said with a crooked smile. "But sometimes a helping hand can improve its chances."

Monika felt her face grow hot and red. Her brow was already covered in sweat and her short hair clung to the back of her neck. She gritted her teeth. She felt like the garmound mother about the roar and snarl at the lazy man.

"It's all for a greater cause," Dasco said, trying to sound reassuring. "I need the pup, and the lefths were a means to that end."

It was as good a confession as Monika ever expected to get. But her jurisdiction ended at the capitol city limits and certainly didn't extend to a jungle somewhere in the multiverse.

"Greater cause?! Means to an end?!" Monika shouted. It startled some wildlife in the canopy of the forest but she didn't care. "A hundred-sixteen people are dead, maybe more by now. You put me, my family, my friends, an entire planet at risk."

She marched up to Dasco on his comfy seat on the stool. His white hair was damp and beads of sweat covered the skin of his bald crown. Swee Pip dragged Rungson's body onto some leaves more focused on that task than Dasco's confession or Monika's anger.

"You and Rungson are more disconnected than any politician I've ever heard of or met," Monika continued. "You think life is meaningless. As abstract as money and as disposable as a napkin. It's not! It's literally my world." Her voice broke and she tried to hide it with more frustration and shouting. "Everything I ever have and ever will experience. Everyone I know is on that planet. And a hundred-sixteen of them are dead because you needed something."

Her anger was doing little to hide the catch in her voice that would soon turn to sobs if she didn't keep up this rant. She could yell at this man all day if she had to. But he'd just do the same thing in some other mortal's backyard. Unaware of the pain on the faces of the victim's family and friends. But she'd seen that pain up close and personal too many times to see life as trivial.

"What do you need? What was worth that price?" She shouted.

"My life," Dasco said.

"You're immortal! I've seen your dead body," Monika said. "A thousand lives across the multiverse isn't enough for you?" Before she knew what she was doing she'd slapped the old man across the face.

Dasco fell off the toadstool and lay on the ground in the same bent seated position. His arm was still wrapped up in the pitcher plant that was now bent over like a wilted flower.

Anyone else in the world would be back on their feet ready to fight her. And she was angry enough to take them on. But Dasco lay there helpless like a man kicked out of a wheelchair. And for a moment Monika was worried her slap had truly hurt him.

Swee Pip finished wrapping Rungson up in leaves and the gar-mound pup circled the cocoon. She helped Dasco back onto the toadstool her sharp talon hands were more gentle with him than Monika thought he deserved. But it was clear something was wrong with him and Swee Pip was playing nurse for these two bastards.

Once Dasco was sitting up Monika noticed his face seemed wilted where she'd slapped him, like it was paralyzed from a stroke.

"He's sick," Swee Pip said. "The holly-lopper on his arm helps, but he's getting worse."

"Then just die." Monika spat the words out. Her anger still out-weighed her sympathy. "Give us mortals a break from being your pawns."

"I would," Dasco said, his words were slurred and slow but prob-ably genuine. "But I know something that can't be forgotten."

Knowledge as a bargaining chip. She'd seen gangsters use it a dozen times. And every time it got them off the hook she lost a little bit of faith in Griffith's justice system. There wasn't anything this man could say that would let her forgive him for the risk and death he'd brought to Griffith.

"What's so important?" Monika asked. Still a detective. Still interested in getting clues.

"Todd's lives are controlled by a puppeteer," Dasco said. "But I know where in the shadows he hides."

23

Gretchen sat on the bench of the escape pod. The whole room was as big as a walk-in closet. It looked and felt like a life raft she'd find on a cruise ship. It was just big enough to hold a dozen people on the plastic benches that lined the white wall.

It got tighter towards the front, away from the airlock she'd entered from. Whoever sat there would probably touch knees with the person across from them. There were no steering controls and two pointless portholes showed the inky black night sky.

Technically it wasn't night, or the sky, but Gretchen needed comfort right now, and thinking of how small she was in the universe would not calm her down.

The room hardly smelled like sewage. The computer was able to keep the air supply separate from the escape pod. Gretchen still had the baggy space suit on and the metal oxygen tank was wheeled into the capsule. She wasn't wearing the little plastic mask, it hung off the metal tank and she stared at it.

"You're going to have to go back in there." The voice was hollow and airy. It sounded like it took Todd everything he had to say it.

And Gretchen ignored it.

Because she was in the escape pod *alone*. There wasn't a decrepit old version of Todd with long thin white hair and flesh that seemed to be sagging off the bones underneath it sitting across from her.

She looked up to check.

Todd gave her a toothy smile. Or at least a smile that would be toothy if he had more than three.

Well, that was that. She'd gone insane. It was bound to happen eventually. Can't travel the multiverse without some consequences. And apparently dreaming about yourself dying countless times was only the admission fee. Concessions cost extra.

"You're not crazy," Todd said. His voice was younger, higher pitched, and energetic. A little boy now sat across from her. Straight brown hair, pudgy cheeks, and feet that barely reached the floor. "You just left before I could finish things."

"Finish what? Killing me again?" she shouted the questions at the boy.

"Mrs. Smith, are you okay?" The computer asked over the intercom of the shuttle.

She rubbed her left wrist nervously. She could feel her grandmother's bracelet under the baggy folds of the suit. The fabric crinkled incessantly like foil as she rubbed it. But she didn't stop.

"I'm fine. Don't launch the escape shuttle," she said. She'd told the computer this a half dozen times. She still didn't trust it to listen. Too many Galaxy Gang episodes centered around rogue computers doing something against the character's will. Todd, her Todd not the one that haunted her, always called it cheap writing. A place where he could see the strings of the puppet master.

"I'm not trying to kill you," Todd said. "I'm helping."

She didn't have to look up to know what age he was at. That voice was familiar. He was maybe thirty or forty. Probably wore the long leather jacket of the monster. Scruffy stubble on his cheeks.

She kept staring at the oxygen tank. Bright green on the background of the white shuttle. "Don't lie to me."

"I'm not," he said. "We don't lie to each other."

A foot leaned on the oxygen tank. It was hairy, the toenails needed to be clipped, and the brown thong of a flip-flop separated the big toe from the rest.

She looked up. The rest of her Todd was there too. Baggy shorts with lots of pockets and a t-shirt that said "I'm here for the fairy cake not a sense of perspective." And his face. It had his long dark beard as thick and messy as the hair on his head. He'd grown the beard one winter in college and just never shaved again. Partially because he hated wasting time shaving, partially because with it he looked as different from her nightmares as possible.

She wanted to leap across the capsule and hug him, be held by him, and complain about the ridiculousness of this space station.

He put a hand up to stop her. "It'll ruin your immersion," he said.

"Are you still the old man? Just putting on his face to trick me?" She asked. He was using the words they'd use at a convention. He dressed in clothes that the monster, and most other people, wouldn't be caught dead in.

"Yes and no," he said. "I'm constructing this from memory, your memory. Which means I can't do anything you wouldn't believe he'd do. Including lies."

"Gods help me," Gretchen said. She'd met a few and doubted any would show up to help now. "Fine. I'll talk. What are you? Why did you attack me?"

This was the part of the show where a good villain monologue would give her, the heroine, the clue she'd need to be free of this ghoul.

"I don't know," Todd said. "I could be a ghost, but that doesn't make sense given it's a few billion years after my death. It could be a side effect of the veins that are attached to your head. I might be–"

"Stop," Gretchen said. Her Todd could've gone on for hours talking and exploring ideas, she wouldn't even have to nod in agreement to keep him going. Which meant the thing was right, it couldn't lie and would do what the memory of her Todd would do.

"Computer, I'm experiencing a side effect from the machine. Hallucinations of Todd. Is that in any of the manuals he sent over?"

"Negative," the computer responded after a second of computation. "His bouts of insanity centered around a hyper fixation on minute details, parallelization from the overwhelming size of the multiverse, jumbled memories, and an inability to recall what he'd consider basic information like language and how to install indoor plumbing."

"Great," Gretchen groaned and rubbed her face. "You can access my memories, and create illusions, but don't know what you are. What did you want to finish?"

"Wiping your memories," Todd said with a demonic smile that her Todd would never use.

"Of course!" Gretchen said. "The thing I want can only be delivered to me by the creepiest thing possible. For once could I do something in this multiverse without being traumatized?!"

"I wouldn't count on it," Todd's voice had gone airy and he was back to the old decrepit version. As creepy as it was Gretchen was glad he wasn't tarnishing the memories of her Todd. A lifetime with him didn't feel like long enough.

Gretchen remembered back to her orientation. The wooden library, the tour by Woah Te, the glowing orb. That was what she wanted out. She didn't want to become debilitated and monstrous like the time-traveling Todd that'd sprung this ability on her.

"I see it now," Todd said. "The memory you want gone."

"Don't take more than you have to," she said. "And don't you dare touch my life with my Todd."

"I wouldn't dream of it," he said with an insane smile.

This was worse than putting the monster's memories in her head. She now had a monster poking around in hers.

"Did you do that to Todd?" she asked. "Take too many of his memories. Make him lose his sense of perspective on the universe." That was the benefit of a perfect memory, according to the avians, infinite generosity and gratitude for all life across the multiverse because you'd lived so many.

However, the way they showed that generosity and gratitude left Gretchen with some questions on the details.

Was her freedom from them worth losing the memory of her life with her Todd. It might ruin her heartfelt nature. Or ruin her optimism despite the terrors that happened to her, and continued to happen.

"Don't worry. I've learned a lot since then," decrepit Todd replied.

She pulled the plastic mask into her hand using the clear tube. The ghoul's answer was far from a ringing endorsement. But the alternative was hanging out with it inside this cramped shuttle until the memory machine decomposed. And potentially never getting free from the avians.

There was an infinite number of Todds throughout the multiverse. But only one was hers. She'd thought this a thousand times, whenever she met someone that had a hint of her Todd's personality in them.

The memory of her Todd was littered throughout her mind. She couldn't forget him even if this ghoul wiped out her entire life with him.

24

I t smelled like someone was cutting up greens for a salad. I couldn't
see anything and I was being smothered by a rigid blanket. My arm
ached but I no longer felt like my skeleton was trying to escape out of
my wrist.

I coughed wet phlegm against whatever was so close to my face.
Barking outside mimicked my cough. I pressed against the rigid covering and it was easy to break from.

I had been inside a burrito of massive leaves. A bushy jungle surrounded me. The air was hot and wet, almost worse than it had been
when I was in the burrito.

The garmound pup crawled over the broken leaves and opened
her mouth in every direction covering my face with her creepy worm
tongues. If I hadn't already learned she was harmless I would've been
terrified.

Swee Pip knelt down next to me. Her large black wings shaded me
from the little bit of light that leaked in from the canopy above me. She
inspected my arm, asked me a few questions about how I felt, and filled
me in on how the lefths had injured me. And the fact that traveling
with the garmound meant my possessions were maintained.

Which explained the shredded leather jacket that was causing me to overheat in the jungle's humidity. I stood up, shrugged it off, and considered taking off my pants too. Seemed inappropriate... but it wasn't off the table if we were sticking around here for long.

"Be careful," Swee Pip said. She seemed worried at my movements. "Your arm is not fully healed."

Dasco stood across from me leaning against a tree. His shirt was un-buttoned and covered in dirt on one side. He looked more disheveled than I'd ever seen him. Even in the hooded sweatshirt, he looked more professional than now.

Pikowski leaned against a tree as far away from Dasco as possible without being in the thick underbrush around us. She switched her gaze between me and Dasco. She scowled at him from across the clearing and then looked concerned and confused at me. But once it seemed like I'd be alright she just reverted to scowling at both of us.

"Thanks for saving me," I said to her in an attempt to break the ice. "I wouldn't have gotten here without you." Not that I knew where here was. Or how we'd gotten here. I hoped Pikowski hadn't learned how to travel in the time I was out. I wouldn't forgive myself.

Hell, she probably wouldn't forgive me. And I could only handle having so many time-traveling women mad at me.

"Your buddy over there is the one that led the lefths to Griffith," Pikowski said.

It was clear she was mad, but my gut reaction was to shrug it off. A few hundred people dying on a planet of a few billion. It was a rounding error. But I was supposed to care about things like that. Life was sacred, apparently. Gretchen would want me to. Both of them.

"God damn it Dasco. Why the hell would you do that?" I asked.

My words were angry but obviously something in my tone gave away that I wasn't because Dasco just shrugged and grabbed his cane from under a pile of his clothes.

"He says he's got information on a puppet master that's controlling your lives," Pikowski said. "And you wouldn't help him with the garmound without motivation."

Tattle-tailing wasn't a great look on her but it made sense considering she was a cop. And the information she'd gotten was interesting. When experiencing my past lives in the mother tree I had noticed a figure guiding my actions. It was an ephemeral interaction and hard to quantify but I'd felt it. Just didn't know what to do about it. Maybe Dasco did.

"Next time just come to me without killing me or anyone else and we can talk this out," I told him. It felt like scolding my grandfather, but who knew which one of us was actually older.

"If there is a next time," Dasco replied.

And he was right. He looked in rough shape beyond just the clothes. He leaned heavily on his cobra cane, his face was inexpressive on one side, and his words were slow and slurred.

"And it's 'bout time we find out if this dog'll hunt," Dasco said pointing to the pup at my heels. And with the slow speech and disheveled shirt, it felt like I was seeing behind the disguise of an industrialist and able to spot the tired rancher underneath.

"How do I know you two aren't going to do something like that again?" Pikowski asked. "Are there any reassurances I can get to know Griffith isn't going to be infested with some other monster next week?"

"Not particularly," Dasco said. "Acts of god and all that."

Pikowski's face turned beet red.

"We won't do anything to Griffith again," I said jumping in to reassure her. "I want to work to make it better."

"Why don't you just leave it alone." Pikowski spat the suggestion at me.

"Ok," I said. "You send out those files I told you about and I never step foot on Griffith again. I can do some time travel tomfoolery and put you in charge as soon as you get back." I considered adding the caveat that this depended on Griffith not being a lefth-infested wasteland, but it seemed counterproductive to my point.

"Ok," Pikowski said. And she sounded like an amateur gambler calling a bluff. "If that's what it takes to keep people safe I'll do it."

Unfortunately for her, I wasn't bluffing.

"I can take her back," Swee Pip said. "You two need to hurry. The holly lopper has done everything it can for him but the parasites are stronger."

The avian reached out her yellow talons for Pikowski to grab them. She'd nursed both me and Dasco back to health as best she could. One day soon I needed to ask her how she avoided being an asshole since it was clear that Dasco and I weren't doing a fantastic job on our own.

"Thank you," I said. "Both of you. I wouldn't be here without you."

Pikowski's scowl softened a bit as she nervously took Swee Pip's claw-like hand. They were gone in an instant.

"Can we get on with this now?" Dasco said, obviously impatient even if his speech was slow. I couldn't blame him considering the circumstances.

"You gonna tell me more about this puppeteer Pikowski mentioned?" I asked.

"Consider it further motivation for you to keep me alive," he said.

"No wonder I wiped our friendship from my mind," I said. "With friends like you who needs enemies?"

The words came out harsher than I meant. But Dasco wasn't fazed by them and continued the explanation of his plan. "The pup can transport inanimate objects, things without conscious bodies, if we can connect ourselves to her through something inanimate she will be able to pull us through time towards you. And she obviously has your scent."

She did indeed. Some of her black fur had darker splotches on them which I could only assume was my blood. Plus she hadn't left my side since standing up from the leaves. There was yet another attachment that I worried I couldn't reciprocate.

"How do we get her to go search for me?" I asked Dasco as he pulled his black tie out of a pile of clothes and tied a knot in it. "It's not like I'm some lost child we're sending a bloodhound after. I'm right here."

Dasco tugged on the knot he'd made. Nothing slipped and it was just big enough to fit over the pup's head if she kept her mouth closed. Unfortunately, she wasn't interested in being calm around Dasco and hissed at him swapping her jaw from opening horizontally to vertically and back. It was uncomfortable to watch. And the man gave up.

"You do it," he said shoving his tie into my hand and leaning exhausted on his cane.

I had no problem picking the pup up and slipping the tie over her head. With a few scratches behind her ear holes, I set her back down holding the thick end of the thin tie in my hand.

"As for how we're going to get her to find you," Dasco said leaning on my shoulder with his free hand. "I'm going to take us to when I last saw you."

25

I stood next to Dasco in front of a wooden door. Nothing fancy just something you'd find at the end of a hallway in an old house. There was shouting on the other side of the door. One voice was clearly Dasco's the other one I couldn't place despite it being familiar.

Dasco and I were still missing our jackets. The garmound pup perched on my shoulder somehow transporting herself there on the trip. Her tentacles wrapped around my arm and shoulder. The tie hung from her neck like she was a toddler trying on her father's clothes. She squawked a delayed roar next to my ear, and Dasco hushed her.

The stranger announced his departure with a huff and the Dasco next to me opened the wooden door.

We entered his parlor. The ornate rug was on the ground. Paintings of landscape hung on the wall. Two burgundy armchairs faced each other in the center of the room. The room smelled like dark tea and tobacco smoke. And the light blue striped wallpaper was peeling at the edges, something I hadn't noticed on my first visit.

The Dasco that was in the room, in his bowler hat and suit, sat in the armchair that faced the door. He had a pipe in his hand and it was as white as the hair of his mustache. Smoke lingered out of it and into the air.

I followed the disheveled Dasco as he limped into the room and towards the armchairs. "We'll be out of your hair in a moment," he said shooing any questions the the younger version of himself was about to throw at him.

It didn't do much good.

"Like hell!" Dasco said, standing up from his armchair. "You owe me answers Todd," he jabbed his pipe at me as I approached the empty armchair.

"He does," my Dasco said slowly and it seemed the younger one finally caught on to how rough of shape he was in. "I'm working on it. I'd tell you I'll give you answers soon, but I never do."

"That doesn't bode well for us," Dasco replied.

"No. It doesn't," my Dasco leaned on the vacant armchair. "But obviously you find him." He gestured at me with his cane. "So get to work." He dismissed his younger self away using the pommel of his cane.

Belligerently Dasco took a drag on his pipe. He blew a cloud of smoke in my direction and before it was all exhaled he'd disappeared.

"I hate taking orders from myself," Dasco told me.

I stood next to him worried that he'd fall over despite the support of the chair under his hand.

"Tell the pup to follow your scent from here," he said resting a hand on my shoulder to make sure our conscious bodies were connected for whatever traveling we were about to do.

So, the unfamiliar voice was me. Lifetimes with the same voice and I still didn't recognize it outside my own head.

I patted the back of the couch then the seat hoping the garmound would follow my hand there. She didn't. Her tentacles were linked around my arm and shoulder holding her in place.

"She's not stupid," Dasco said. "Just tell her what you want."

"Follow my scent," I said in a sing-song voice. I felt ridiculous. I don't like pets for this reason. Bees don't need you to talk all cutesy to them they take care of themselves.

"You think she knows Common Tongue?" Dasco said, clearly frustrated. "She senses and works with consciousness. Communicate with that."

"Like telepathy?"

"Like charades," Dasco said. "Act it out from your conscious body. Like you really mean it, otherwise it won't come through clearly to her."

I took a deep focused breath like I was going to travel but didn't pick a location. I took another breath aimlessly focusing out on the void of time. It was clear this parlor was outside of the astral plane and a real place in the multiverse since I could feel the fraying of timelines around me.

I looked at the garmound on my shoulder then did a comically overacted searching look. Her emerald eyes showed some sort of recognition. She gave a little roar and we were out of the parlor.

She jumped off my shoulder and onto a metal floor. I caught the tie as she rushed down the hallway of the Fortress of Solitude. Dasco had a hard time keeping up and I put my aching arm under his shoulder as the pup strained against the loop at the end of the tie.

We entered the center atrium as a man disappeared from the chair at the desk of monitors.

The garmound transported us across the room. She appeared in the chair and buried her conical nose into the cushion. Her tentacles flailed wildly in the air excited by the chase.

I held onto the tie in my hand that connected me to her. Dasco was under my other arm, leaning on me more than his cane. He looked faint. I hoped this pup could get us there in time to help him.

A roar echoed through the space station. It reverberated off the metal walls. It was far too loud for the pup to let out.

Her mother was on our trail.

We appeared on a rocky ledge. Ice-cold wind whipped around us and for once I wished I had my jacket. Mountains rose up into ominous green clouds. It was day, but the clouds blocked the sun out leaving everything in a puke-green tint.

The garmound pulled on the tie as she walked up the mountain. There was a trail made of gravel and it weaved through tall spike pillars that seemed to grow out of the mountains.

Dasco shivered in the wind. His shirt was still unbuttoned. His cane fell out of his hand as the pup yanked me around a corner, but I didn't have the strength to go back for it without letting go of the eager pup.

A roar was carried on the wind. The large garmound knocked over rocky spires as it barreled down the narrow gravel path. The pup seemed unfazed by it. I sweat bullets despite the chilly wind.

At the opening of a cave, the garmound stopped and sniffed around in circles. Inside the cave a fire ring filled with dying embers and a few piles of supplies. I wanted to dig through the supplies. See what clues I might find. But the garmound mother would be on us in a second and the pup had her scent.

We appeared in the living room of a suburban home.

Sun streamed in through the large windows. The walls were painted off-white, a few family photos were hanging on them. I didn't recognize the family, or anyone in them. If one of them was me I must've been wearing a face I didn't remember. That was always an uncomfortable process, but sometimes it was nice to not be yourself.

The garmound weaved through the house taking us to a room near the back of the house. The house must have been empty because no one bothered us. We weren't quiet.

The roar behind our entry and the crashing sound of walls being torn down in the mother's hunt didn't hide her presence either.

The garmound pup nosed her way through the partially closed door. It was an office. Boxes were stacked everywhere. A boxy computer and monitor sat on a small desk. The garmound sniffed the boxes, interested in whatever was inside. If I had a free hand, and time, I would've opened one for her.

Dasco's breath was faint. He hadn't said anything, not even a groan, in the past few minutes.

The door burst off its hinges and crashed into the desk. The garmound mother had shoved her face into the room. Her body was too wide to get to us but her tongues reached out for me.

Her breath reeked of rot and death. And I knew if they wrapped around me I would be gone for good.

26

The pup transported us to a dirt-floored warehouse. The thudding of a heart echoed through the room, for a moment I thought it was my own.

We'd found the purple heart machine that was delivered to me. If I'd known this was what we were looking for I would've brought Dasco to it sooner. It was sitting in the Fortress of Solitude at some point in Griffith's future.

But for some reason whoever wiped my memory didn't see fit to leave that information in. Which was enough to clear Dasco from the suspect list.

Plus he was looking worse for the wear. He needed immediate attention.

He slipped out of my arms and onto the dirt floor. My arm ached from carrying him. He wasn't a big guy, but carrying anyone for that long was tough. And Swee Pip had said my arm wasn't done healing. How I strained wasn't clear. But the pain was.

A blue man who looked like he was cut out of cardboard walked up to us and kneeled down next to Dasco.

"He needs help," I said. "Can that thing wipe memories?" I asked. I didn't have time to process the strange humanoid offering his help. I was just glad I wasn't in this alone anymore.

The man replied but it was buried under a loud roar.

I let go of the pup's tie. I hoped this was our final destination because the mother would soon be getting her pup and likely me.

The doors to the dirt-floored warehouse were large enough to let her in. The warehouse was full of boxes, supplies, breakable equipment, and tools. One swipe of the garmound's paw could destroy plenty of valuable equipment. Equipment I'd likely need if I wanted answers.

I rushed out of the warehouse hoping that she wouldn't be interested in Dasco or the strange two-dimensional man.

The pup followed the tie dragging in the dirt behind her.

The garmound mother appeared in front of me. Her face looked down on me, her mossy green eyes were full of fury. She roared again and opened her mouth in every direction. Her tentacles and tongues reached out for me.

I'd stolen her pup and this was the retaliation I deserved. Based on the damage the lefths did to my arm I could only imagine what destruction this beast could unleash.

I stood weaponless, in a bright grass field surrounded by hills spotted with black boxy houses.

The mother's tentacles latched onto my arms and I knew I would die under this strange purple sky.

Her tentacles pulled my arms in opposite directions. They both burned and it was difficult to tell which one was the injured one, and if she was making it worse.

She certainly wasn't making it better.

The massive hound stretched me out in front of her mouth, unwilling to give me a chance to disappear.

Not that my disappearance would do any good. She'd found me here. I had no way to get back to Dasco's safely insulated Pearlescent City. She'd find me anywhere else I went. Meaning wherever I went I'd bring her destruction in my wake.

And this planet I'd landed on was no exception. The strange cardboard people of this world began forming a crowd on a hill beyond us.

Maybe the garmound would destroy them anyway. The first time I'd come here the buildings were overgrown and the garmound was hunting a flock of teleporting birds. Not a cardboard soul in sight.

I hoped revenge on me would get the mother to leave this planet alone for a few million years. Keep its occupants safe.

I didn't know these citizens. At least didn't remember knowing them. And somehow that anonymity made causing their Armageddon worse.

I didn't want that to be my legacy. Not that I was in a position to negotiate.

But there was one thing I could do.

Dasco said garmounds were smart and could be communicated with. Just not in Common Tongue. But maybe I could appeal to her with my conscious body. Even though I had my doubts about how forgiving a mother would be for abducting her child.

I bent my knees and I would've fallen down if the tentacles weren't holding me up. Nearly kneeling on the coiled grass below me I looked past the tooth-filled mouth and into the dark green eyes of the garmound mother.

I pleaded with my eyes. Tried to fill them with sorrow, a habit I'd grown callus to over my lifetimes.

I reached out with my mind trying to find the cave I'd abducted her pup from. Not to escape, merely to convince her to do her business there, not around this budding society.

I apologized, in blabbering words and pleading gestures. My arms strained against her strong tentacles. Not to escape but to make my point.

Dasco said while it may seem like charades with my conscious body I'd have to mean it. Otherwise, my message wouldn't go through clearly.

It felt like I was giving a dissertation in a foreign language with only a tourist's dictionary for reference.

The snake-like tongues reaching out for my face made it clear I wasn't doing a great job.

Small yips cut through the mother's roar. They were far away at first. Then deafening as the pup appeared on my shoulder.

The pup's small tentacles swatted away at the mother's tongue keeping them away from my face. She began to gnaw at one of the tentacles around my arm snarling and scowling and her mother. She had a dark rebellious look in her eyes despite her bright emerald irises.

The blows were likely as harmless to her mother as they had been to my hand when I first picked her up.

But they did something because the mother dropped me to the ground. My face landed on the mossy grass.

I scrambled onto my back to see the pup wrapped up in her mother's tentacle the long tail of the black tie fluttering in the wind.

The mother growled at me, deep, angry, and resentful.

Then she disappeared.

My heart thud in my chest. My breath was uneven panting. My whole body shook with nervous shivers. I couldn't get up from the ground. I stared at the purple sky.

"Todd," the flat man said lifting me up from the ground with his boxy arms. "You need to attend to your friend."

27

A half dozen cardboard people were circled around Dasco and the machine. New machines had been set up and were beeping away. And none of the beeps were happening at a reassuring tempo.

None of the crayon-blue cardboard people were taller than my chest. I approached and looked over them. With all the medical equipment I half expected to see Dasco lying cut open on an emergency room operating table.

What I actually saw was much worse.

Veins and arteries wrapped around his face and chest holding him in place on the inclined bench. They'd weaved their way into his nose and ears and anywhere else they could take root. It looked like he was being absorbed into the machine.

Fluid pumped through the veins at the rhythm of the purple heart behind him. The metal structures that held the organs in place were wrapped up just as much as Dasco.

The only thing connected to the machine that wasn't covered in veins was the thick computer monitor and a keyboard with a familiar key mapping.

"What's going on with him?" I asked the cardboard man that led me inside. If he was the same one who greeted me on my arrival I couldn't tell.

"We're wiping the parasitic dream as you instructed us," the man said. His voice was high-pitched and sounded like wet rubber soles squeaking on tile. "But we're worried it's too late to help him."

"Don't worry, he won't die." A human voice said this. If I hadn't heard it shouting at Dasco a few minutes ago I wouldn't have recognized it.

I turned around and saw a version of myself standing behind me. The one that'd built this whole machine. He wore my leather trench coat, a black shirt, and jeans that had significantly less blood and rips on them than my current pair. Instead, these had dark oily stains on them. His beard was longer than the two-day scruff that I normally had when I traveled, meaning he'd been here a while and hadn't traveled to appear in the warehouse.

"You want to explain what's going on here?" I asked him. Surely he knew more than me, he was the one who'd wiped most of what I knew out of my head. Including this encounter.

"Dasco won't die," he said wading through the crowd of people surrounding his friend. He placed an arm on the man's shoulder. "But I don't expect him to wake up either."

"I know he's not going to be plugged into this machine forever," I said. "So what's going to happen to him?"

"This machine will remove the memory that helps the parasites locate him. Meaning they won't break down his Pearlescent City. However, they've left his conscious body too weak to reconsolidate."

"Sounds a lot like dying to me," I said. It was what Dasco had just explained a few days earlier, ages ago. Our physical bodies are made of atoms that break down. Our conscious bodies break down to make new conscious beings. Dasco was worried the parasites would destroy the Pearlescent City, but that couldn't stay standing if his conscious body dispersed.

"If my research is correct, or at least the references Swee Pip gave me are correct, he will crystallize in his astral form because of his connection to it."

"That's a big if," I said. I was unclear on the crystallizing and astral form bit. And quite frankly I had bigger concerns on my mind. "I have this machine on the Fortress. If you hadn't wiped its purpose from our mind I could've brought Dasco to it sooner."

The bearded version of myself nodded a solemn nod. "I needed to get you here without attracting attention. Dasco is good at that kind of travel. Always has been."

"It's going to cost him his life!"

He nodded with a frown. "Effectively yes. He will be locked in place as the Pearlescent City in the astral plane. Unable to move but still able to tend to his beasts and visitors as he always enjoyed. It's a sacrifice my friend has made for us. I told him I was grateful for it."

These two bastards were always throwing away other people's lives for their own. Seeing it come back around on Dasco didn't make it any easier.

Machines beeped. We both stared at Dasco. The blue people had hobbled away taking care of other work in the warehouse.

"So we need to make his death worth it," he finally said breaking the silence between us.

"There's things in his head that we need to know," I said. "He knows where our puppeteer is." The words didn't make sense to me but they might make sense to a version of myself with more memories.

The look of shock and surprise he gave me signaled I'd struck a chord. He jumped on the computer and started typing frantically away.

Dasco groaned under the weight of whatever was being done at the terminal. His eyes crunched up adding more wrinkles around them. The purple heart beat faster. The veins that encased Dasco pulsed and seemed to tighten around him like a boa constrictor.

If I hadn't been staring at Dasco I would've missed it. The other version of me didn't see a thing, too focused on the screen in front of him.

Dasco's body shattered into a hundred pieces like a clay pot. The veins caved in with nobody to hold them up. The tiny shards of him turned to dust like ash from a fire. Then the few pieces I could track seemed to fall away from me. But they didn't move towards the ground or the bench. They seemed to sink down in a fourth direction I couldn't perceive.

The version of me at the terminal let out a dozen curses. I looked on in awe of the death that had just transpired in front of me.

I'd seen countless people die. I'd been the cause of a majority of them. Dasco's death was like no other. I felt light-headed. The warehouse seemed to spin around me despite standing as still as stone.

I was mortal. Dasco had been mortal. He'd been destroyed. Meaning I could be destroyed too.

At one point in time, that'd be a relief. Right now it terrified me.

"Nothing!" The other version of me said slamming his hand on the keyboard letting out a plastic clatter. "Not a goddamn thing."

I finally broke down and laughed. Not at the tormented version of myself. Not at the shock of Dasco's death. But at how our friend had pulled one over on us for the final time. He got the last laugh, but he wasn't here to chuckle.

"You threw him away like an old newspaper," I said. "You didn't realize winning lottery numbers were written inside."

"You think this was an easy choice for me?" He whirled away from the terminal and looked at me. We were technically the same height but his anger made him seem taller. "He is our oldest friend. Older than both of us. Combined. He helped us in and out of dozens of tight spots. If he's right he'll help us out of a dozen more before this is all over."

"If he's so important why wipe him from my mind?" I asked eager to get some answers. Hell, I'd download the answers from the machine if I had to.

"That wasn't an easy decision either," he said. "But memories are how the puppeteer pulls the strings. I deleted them. Most of them. And the ones I saved shouldn't be accessed until the strings are cut for good."

"What's this puppeteer thing we're trying to escape?" I asked.

"The puppeteer guides our actions through all our lifetimes. Not by telling us what to do but by setting up initial conditions in each multiverse to lead us to his desired outcome. We think our choices are our own. But he's pulling the strings."

"Why escape the puppeteer at all?" I asked. "What's so bad about him pulling the strings?" Being able to blame someone else for my mistakes seemed like a weight off my shoulders and not a bad deal.

"Because of what he makes us do. I've seen it. It can't be avoided. I've cut the strings for now. But we need to go further. We need to tie him into the destruction he causes.

"But he'll see us coming if we're not careful. The planning and plotting in these pockets of time where his eyes aren't on us are key to catching him flat-footed."

"What plans?!" I was frustrated by this version of myself. "You've destroyed or hidden them. How is that a success?"

"I've set some initial conditions of my own," he said to me. A twisted smirk crawled across his face. "If things go right we'll pull enough strings to get him wrapped up in the destruction he drives us to. But if I tell you now the links will be too obvious. You're better off, safer, finding them on your own."

"Not playing the game at all seems like a better choice than trying to outsmart this shadowy grandmaster," I said.

"He showed me the destruction we caused. That conclusion is set in stone. We'll scar entire multiverses before we're done."

"I've caused enough pointless destruction already. Why not take us off the table completely." I gestured to where Dasco's body would've been if he'd died a normal death.

"We both have. Get over it. Only a narcissist wants you to mourn them forever. We must move our sights to repairing the damage. And the puppeteer can't see past his shadows. He can't see the potential he's given us."

He pressed a key on the computer a horrible squelching sound echoed through the warehouse. But I couldn't turn my eyes off of this madman and his ravings.

Ever since I met the avians on the Mother Tree I'd assumed I'd lost my mind. Now it was clear I never had a great grasp of it to begin with.

"We must keep our visits to this planet secret. I can get you to the space station incognito," he said gesturing at the machine he was about to ship there. "I've put two memories in this machine. The second one will give you some answers. But most importantly stay hidden when you travel."

"How the hell am I supposed to do that?" If I hadn't wiped my damn memory then maybe I'd know how. But someone didn't think that information seemed fit to leave in.

"Necklaces, or any astral artifact, can conceal your movement. Dasco prefers those. Latching onto others will conceal you, but finding someone reliable to travel with is difficult. I'm hoping I can remedy that by getting us another friend. Taming conscious-bodied beasts is harder, as you demonstrated outside. The best thing to do is to not travel at all. Ride out the stream of time. Which is what you're going to do here."

"How? We still age. Unless you've got a fix to that." Considering the strange mix of rudimentary and advanced infrastructure these hobbling cardboard humanoids had I wouldn't be shocked if he had found a solution.

"By merging your conscious body with the machine's." He walked past the computer and towards the heart.

I hadn't noticed it over the beeping of the machines and our conversation but the heart had stopped beating. It was cracked open like a pecan. The large ventricle cavities were wet with purple blood.

"Take a seat," he said gesturing to the cavities in the machine. "You'll be home before you know it."

28

Gretchen sat back on the bench of the machine. The room smelled of sewage and the plastic mask was wearing an indent on the bridge of her nose. The cord that connected her to the metal tank floated in the null gravity of the shuttle.

She was going to get these last two memories out of the machine. And hopefully, the machine, or this illusion of Todd, would get the avian tracking memory out of her.

The white wiry-haired version of Todd hunched over her as she felt veins crawl around her forehead, neck, and face. She gagged as they wiggled down her nose.

She stood in an office full of boxes. The body was uncomfortable partially because it wasn't hers and partially because the memory remembered it being uncomfortable. She could taste garlic mashed potatoes and the room smelled like cigarettes.

Strangely everything was silent.

An old boxy monitor, similar to the one on the machine, sat on a small desk. Sheets of paper were laid out on the floor. Bookshelves lined the walls, mostly filled with stone statues and wood carvings, and not a lot of books. A small window in the corner showed it was dark outside.

The person controlling her body, she assumed it was Todd, looked at each of the pieces of paper carefully. Some were written in English, but most were written in Common Tongue, a language from the future that she had far from mastered. She recognized a few cognates but the rest were undecipherable.

However, it wasn't nearly as bad as the minimalist curved language on the rest of the papers. She recognized it, but only because she'd spent so much time in the Mother Tree with the avians. They hadn't shared how to read or speak it with her.

Although Todd, the one controlling her body, seemed to be able to understand all three languages. But whatever memory of speaking the language wasn't stored here in this snapshot of a memory.

He pointed to bits that were important, with hands that weren't familiar. She felt her mouth move, but could not hear the sounds.

A woman entered the room dressed in an apron and a starched dress. Half a cigarette hung from her lips. Smoke lingered to the ceiling. The old hunchbacked version of Todd followed the woman into the room.

Todd stood to shoo her out the door. The old man ignored the gestures.

Gretchen stood in a cave. A cloudy green sky outside. A fire burned on the sandy floor of the cave. Something was scratched into the sand as well. A map. X marked the spot. Using a bent driftwood stick Gretchen's body pointed the way from the cave where they were to the buried treasure. The hands were Todd's now. She'd recognize them anywhere.

She felt her mouth move but still couldn't hear a sound. Not even the whistling of wind or the crackle of the fire.

She turned around and pointed. His hand went right through the shoulder of the decrepit Todd.

The ancient man's wrinkly fingers reached for her face. He wrapped his long fingers around the back of her skull.

Her body began to walk. She could feel gravel through the thick soles of her boots but her steps made no sound. The old man hovered in front of her his toothless grin inches away from her face. He ate away at the avian's orientation memories.

Gretchen could feel them disappearing. It felt like freedom. She'd be able to travel again without the avians watching her every move.

She was standing back in the office. The old white-haired man blocked most of her view. His toothless grin was wicked and crooked. Todd was lifting a relic off of the bookcase. She couldn't see it clearly with this man in her way.

The memory seemed to urge her to pay attention. She knew this was important. But Gretchen couldn't focus.

Gretchen's mind was empty of the orientation. All the important facts the avians gave to her to keep her safe during her travels through the multiverse were gone. All the warnings they'd given her to control her. To keep her doing their bidding were gone.

The ancient man still clung to her head.

She wanted to shout at him to go away. To shoo him. To slap his wrinkly face. She was frozen. Locked into the movements of the memory.

He clung on. Like a parasite.

Then she forgot the name of her high school. Her college. Their mascot and school colors.

He was hungry looking for more.

Gretchen's body was digging through boxes now. How they'd gotten from the bookshelf to there she didn't know. There were a lot of circuit boards and other technology in the boxes. Things far more advanced than she'd ever seen. She didn't understand them.

She felt like she should've. The memories should've. Something was missing. More than just audio.

She didn't care. She wanted the memory to be done with. The machine had done its work. Now it was going rogue.

As her body looked over some schematic for a glowing green orb she didn't understand the old man took away the name of her first dog. The address of the first permanent home she'd bought with her Todd.

From the corner of her eye, she saw Todd burst through the door. He had the face of the monster. Short scruffy beard, a long coat. Her body didn't turn or react. As far as the memory was concerned he wasn't there.

Todd clawed the old man's fingers off the back of her head. Her body didn't react. Her mind was ecstatic for the freedom.

The ancient man fell to the ground but scrambled to his feet faster than a body his age should. He reached for Gretchen again.

The three of them stood in the atrium of the space station. Gretchen typed a code into the computer. 2192420. It was important. She should remember it.

The old man ran for her. Todd, the one who'd shown up and saved her, pushed him back onto the metal floor of the station. It didn't make a sound. They wrestled on the ground silently. The old man reached for her ankles, and Todd fought him away.

The hum of the station's air vents suddenly appeared and was deafening.

"And that should be everything you need to know," she said. It was the first words she'd been able to hear in the memory. They were the least helpful.

Slimy veins slid off of her face and out of her nose. Gretchen sat up panting heavily into the plastic oxygen mask.

There was still a third memory to experience. She didn't know if she could handle it.

"Mrs. Smith what did you do to the machine?" the computer asked.

The room was ice cold. Her baggy space suit insulated her but her cheeks and ears felt frozen solid. The loud ventilation fans that pumped oxygen in and hydrogen sulfide out were nearly deafening.

But the heart was silent.

"The third memory," Gretchen said. "I have to get it." She'd recovered so little information from the machine. The third memory had to have more answers in it. Something she could tell Todd about.

"What third memory?" The computer asked. "The documentation states there should only be two."

Something popped like a balloon and it startled Gretchen. The metal oxygen tank clattered to the ground. Blobs of purple and blue liquid floated above Gretchen. She pulled her ponytail out of the way so it didn't get hit.

She looked at the machine. It was covered in boils and sores. At least the parts of it that were still solid. A few organs had burst and a few veins were leaking dark purple blood.

The large purple heart sat motionless. It was covered in black spots like a moldy fungus. Instead of standing firm and strong like a muscle should it wafted around like a deflated balloon.

It cracked with a wet squelching sound. The bottom of it had given out like a wet paper bag.

A thick-soled boot stuck out. The blue hem of a jean followed.

29

Gretchen pulled on my foot and I floated out of the purple heart. I coughed wet coughs and saliva floated around me. It smelled putrid in here. I wanted to vomit but my stomach was empty. A few million years in hibernation will do that to you.

Gretchen looked up at me. A plastic mask rested on her face, and a ridiculously large space suit covered the rest of her. She pulled me down to her level and placed the mask on my face. I inhaled deeply. It was fresh and sterile air.

Gretchen took the mask back to take a breath for herself.

"Let's get out of here before I vomit," I said.

Gretchen led me to the door, she was the only one of us that had any control in this zero-G shuttle.

My muscles ached under the artificial gravity of the station. The smell didn't improve outside the shuttle. I was still covered in blood, some of it mine, some of it the lefths, some of it belonged to the rotting machine.

"What happened in there?" Gretchen asked as we slowly made our way to the central atrium. I wasn't sure if she meant in the memory, the shuttle, or when I was in the heart. Either way, it'd be a lot to explain.

The computer read off atmosphere percentiles as we made our way to the center atrium. It was currently flooding the whole ship with nitrogen to get the sewage smell out.

Gretchen and I sat on the recessed couches in the center of the station. We traded the oxygen mask back and forth as the station became habitable again. Gretchen slipped out of the bulky space suit and was wearing a royal purple shirt that matched the tattoo around her wrist.

I badly wanted to change into something that wasn't ripped up and covered in blood.

"The machine was infested with parasites," I said. It was an unintended consequence of taking the parasitic memory out of Dasco's mind. The parasites honed in on the machine as a new target. "They've been eating away at the memories stored inside it for ages. They were trying to latch on to you as well."

"And you got them off me, right?" Gretchen looked at her clothes a little disgusted, as if she was worried the parasites would be dancing on the surface.

"They're gone. For good. Along with the memories I was trying to send myself. Whatever's in your head is all we have to work with."

Gretchen gave me a worried frown. "What I got was spotty. Like a corrupted file. Any explanation you were giving me was muted."

I cursed. Then coughed on the putrid air. The fumigation was clearing the air but it still smelled awful.

"I'm sorry," Gretchen said. "But I got the tracking memory out. I'm free to leave without being followed."

Time stood still for a moment. At first, I thought it was the terror of being left alone again. Of Gretchen leaving me alone on this massive station. I hadn't minded it before. But now I had an enemy. A dozen puzzles to solve. And I'd lost my oldest friend, who I only remembered knowing for far too short a time.

Then I realized time had stopped because a void figure was standing across the seating area from me. It was a black humanoid gap in reality. Lanky limbs that came together at a point without fingers or feet.

Gretchen had said she cleared the memory. There shouldn't be a way for the avians to find us. There shouldn't be a way for anyone who doesn't already know about the location of this station to find us. I was supposed to travel here undetected and had done everything I could given the paltry information I was left with.

Another void figure appeared. It sat at the bar above the seating area. It was a seat a void figure had taken before. Before I went off to help Gretchen come to terms with her powers.

If I wasn't frozen I would have panicked, fled, drawn a breath. But maybe that was the trick. They were trying to make me travel, be noticed, and give away my position.

The figure in front of us resolved into an avian with a sleek hawk-like head. Stark black feathers covered her body with the exception of her golden talons, beak, and eyes. A purple sash hung across her chest.

A man appeared at the bar. He took his bowler hat off. The bright overhead lighting glared off the skin of his bald head. He pressed a few buttons, apparently familiar with the controls, and a martini rose out of the bar's countertop.

"It smells rank in here Todd," Dasco said. "Did you try to modify the plumbing again?"

He stepped away from the bar and walked down to the seating area to join us. He didn't use a cane. There was no limp in his step.

"You died," I said.

"Probably will one day. Don't spoil it for me," he said. The little hair he had was still snow white and matched his broom-like mustache. His ice-blue eyes still had wrinkles around them. But somehow, to me, he looked younger.

Gretchen whistled then popped her lips followed by another whistle. Swee Pip responded with a whistle of her own. Gretchen's cheeks turned red, and her shirt faded from purple to pink like an old mood ring.

"You know her?" I asked.

"She's the lost avian princess," Gretchen said. "They've been looking for her for ages."

"And if I keep my nest neat they'll be looking for me for many more seasons," Swee Pip said with a bragging whistle. "Monika sends her regards. She was doing well on Griffith last time I visited her."

That answered my question about where Swee Pip stood in the timeline. "You stayed in touch? She's doing well?" I asked. I needed to get back to Griffith and put her in charge, but there seemed to be no doubt that I would eventually get to it.

"You threw a lot at her," Swee Pip said. "I brought her some reference material as needed. We are good friends now. Although I don't like that Kot fellow. Felines shouldn't be trusted, let alone kept as pets."

The computer dinged with a notification. Something had arrived on the outer ring. "A shipment from Griffith," the computer announced. "The manifest says it's a wardrobe for Mrs. Smith."

Gretchen let out a little cheer.

The stench had cleared from the air. I had a few friends around me. And no shortage of puzzles to solve. But I thought Dasco had the right idea. It was time for a drink.

I walked up to the bar and ordered a whiskey. The finest thing I had stocked wasn't nearly nice enough for the occasion.

As soon as I picked up my drink a roar echoed through the station. The hair on my neck stood on end. The garmound mother hadn't forgiven me after all.

Clomping footsteps echoed down the long hallway of the station. A panther-sized beast with a sharp nose lunged for me. She tackled me to the ground. My glass clattered to the ground spilling.

The garmound split her mouth open and licked my face with her two serpentine tongues. It gave me a splitting headache but that was all the harm it did.

I wrestled her off me. I only succeeded because she let me. Her bright emerald eyes looked up at me, excited for something. Maybe another hunt. There would certainly be a few more in our future.

The pup had grown up. She now stood to my waist. But she had yet to reach the towering stature of her mother. I scratched her behind her ear holes and then down her neck. I massaged between the tentacles of her shoulders as I ordered another drink.

Something soft and silky hung on her right front tentacle. A black necktie that nearly blended into her black fur.

I took it off her. Tied it right but loose. She weaved her conical head inside.

I smiled at the crowd that'd gathered in my space station. I may look a mess but I had sharp friends around me. And now all of them were dressed sharp. Every part of my conscious body was filled with gratitude for their arrival. I wouldn't be able to take on this puppeteer alone.

Also By Nicholas Licalsi

The Slugs of Dale Cannon

Rystole Whitlock, a young rancher and colonists on the Earth-like planet of Dale Cannon, spends his days cutting class and herding buffcows.

When a group of alien slugs invade his family's cabin he can't find a good way to corral them before the toxic slugs put his mother in a coma.

Determined to save his mom, and the rest of the colony, Rystole won't stop until he gets revenge or a cure.

If you enjoy exploring alien worlds and first contact stories with young heroes then you'll enjoy Slugs of Dale Cannon.

https://books2read.com/SlugsOfDaleCannon

The Hacked Manticore and Other Cyberpunk Stories

Bett the hacker gets a personalized message on a computer he just broke into. J-Red the streamer accepts a mobster's job offer to get his belongings out of repo. Pairs of packages and pizzas arrive at the doorstep of recently unemployed Kiran.

The cyberpunk world of Galleria Valley runs on corporate greed, shady mob deals, and bionic enhancements. No one survives long when playing by the rules.

Let these short stories be the neon lights that guide your hovercar through the towering buildings of Galleria Valley.
https://books2read.com/HackedManticore

A Trial of Rock and Rope

Upon his death, Ferrun Monteiro wakes up in the afterlife. Instead of building paradise the gods have designed a challenge.

To escape the afterlife Ferrun must reach the top of a mountain with a boulder tied to his ankle.

Yet not a single soul has completed this seemingly simple trial.

Unperturbed, Ferrun faces the god's challenge head on. Follow him on his odyssey through the afterlife.

If you enjoy dreaming about the afterlife, you'll enjoy A Trial of Rock and Rope.

https://books2read.com/ATrialOfRockAndRope

About the Author

Nicholas Licalsi's love for science fiction and fantasy started with a box of his grandfather's pulp paperbacks and the brainwashing alien parasite nesting between their pages. This led to an interest in engineering, robotics, and time travel.

After a successful enough career in software development Nicholas now spends his time trying to trick his overactive imagination into paying the bills while he satiates his dog's need to be pet.

He currently has 9 independently published books available everywhere books are sold and countless short stories on his blog StepInto TheRoad.com. You can get a free book, and updates about his writing, time traveling, and (most importantly) his dog by signing up for his email list at StepIntoTheRoad.com/SignUp

You can connect with me at: https://stepintotheroad.com

Get updates about my upcoming books at: https://stepintoth eroad.com/signup